Brother, Sister, Mother, Explorer

Catapult  New York

Brother

Sister

Mother

Explorer

A Novel

JAMIE FIGUEROA

Copyright © 2021 by Jamie Figueroa

ISBN: 978-1-948226-88-2

Jacket design by Nicole Caputo
Book design by Wah-Ming Chang

Library of Congress Control Number: 2020936786

Printed in the United States of America
1 3 5 7 9 10 8 6 4 2

*For the community of beloved hands that have
caught and carried me again and again.*

Once there was and was not . . .

—traditional opening line
of Armenian folktales

Contents

Friday

One

"Oh, holy. Holy, holy," sings the sister, Rufina. "My baby. Return." She can skin a refrain until it's raw, a glistening pulp of yearning. Which is to say, she won't be the one who loses. Anyone can sing a song, hum a melody, claim a costume, but the way she tilts toward the crowd with the whole of her body, like a ready-made promise—now, that should get your attention. It's undeniable: she means it. Don't take your eyes off her.

It's the end of May and ten past four on a Friday afternoon. This high desert mountain city has already begun to swell. At the height of the season, Ciudad de Tres Hermanas will double in size, and then some. Tourists pant dry air through open mouths at 7,000 feet, waiting to be fooled. It's dizzying. They have earned this right. Saved up for it.

Never mind them. This is not a story about them, after all. This is a story about Rufina, and her brother, Rafa, who are performing little creatures they call songs, which are not songs at all. Not songs but eruptions of noise. Prayers, fortunes. Let's not call it ridiculous, which it can be if you're not in the mood.

The plaza is a patchwork of grass, anointed with cottonwoods and box elders, pines and Russian olives. Trees are a blessing here in this place where water shamelessly flirts. Decorating the cottonwoods: crows, hungry, and black as regret. Beyond the trees, and the city limits, beyond all the one-story buildings made of mud and dirt and spit, four mountain ranges huddle, one in each direction, as if conspiring. Do you see them? Don't you agree? Their backs toward you, peaks crowned with snow, as if royalty. And the sky, the only enduring commitment, so vast and blue it's no longer blue, no longer sky. The crows bark, a murder of them locked on the umbrella of branches above.

It's as if Rufina is ten, not twenty-eight, and Rafa is twelve, not weeks shy of thirty. This is what the recent death of a mother will do, strip adulthood from grown children. Send them to the streets begging for a reason to live. You'll see. It's Rufina's fault. Blame her if it doesn't work. She's the one who, the previous night, crawled under their deceased mother's bed where Rafa was pretending to hide—as if his filthy feet jutting out from beneath the frame hadn't given him away—and told him, "Look, if you want to die, too, you're going to have to earn it. Life isn't easy and neither is death." Her voice was a constant hiss of air. "You're not going to hang around here dissolving like you're some kind of . . ." Rufina paused, searching for the right word, the right image that would sufficiently support her scolding. All possibilities escaped her.

It had been four months since they covered their mother, Rosalinda—the small, dark worn scrap of her—in a blanket of mums and carried her away to be burned. It had been dusk and the snow had glinted in midair while coyotes split the quiet with their crying. Rafa and Rufina had studied her as her waning hours had passed as if she were a map they would never truly understand.

Rufina inched closer to her brother's face. Leaned toward the fleshy nub of his nose, as if it were a microphone. "It's disgusting," she said. "Get to living or get a weapon. Enough is enough." She hoped her threat would work, hoped she could still manipulate her brother with a healthy dose of shame. Tricky, she knew, but worth a try.

The day after Rosalinda's death, Rafa and Rufina had both lain on the cold tile floor of the living room, neither of them able to will themselves to stand, put match to kindling, and tend a fire that would thaw them. Instead, they remained numb. Grief waited at the edges, sniffing the boundaries of their bodies, waiting to be let in. The house had no choice but to watch.

On the second day after Rosalinda's death, Rufina got up and started the fire.

Rafa remained lost for the third day and the fourth day, the fifth and sixth, staring into space, drifting in and out of sleep. He seemed to prefer the floor, as had his mother. It was where she had stitched embroidery and painted her ink portraits, where she ate and where she sat long hours, staring out the window that stretched from ceiling to floor of the south-facing wall while a record tumbled sound and one cigarette after another clung to her bottom lip.

With each week, then each month, Rafa had lost more weight, paled further, spoke less. Each new day had demanded he persist. He lit one of Rosalinda's cigarette butts, stained with her fuchsia lipstick, and let the smoke fill his nose, laced with the scent of her headache-inducing perfume. He could not get enough of his mother. The woman who was no more.

Under the bed, Rufina was close enough to see the splinters of amber in her brother's wood-colored eyes. "We know how to do this," she said. "Remember how they used to throw money at us?" Which was almost the truth. Nearly a decade and a half before, they had been under the artistic direction of the Explorer. He had arranged the two of them and their mother in the plaza, had them pose for hours. They were his material. His models. The money he collected on their behalf was impressive.

Ultimately, the conversation had been one-sided and brief. In the end, Rufina was able to convince Rafa that pretending would get them just as far as practice. You could do anything in front of a crowd of tourists and get money, she reminded him. There was the way you stared at any of them, as if they were the only tourist that had ever existed; the way you smiled, as if that one and only tourist were desperate to spend money; the way you convinced the disoriented and slightly drunk tourist that they were not only welcome, but belonged. Rufina and Rafa had hours of this kind of performance embedded in their bodies. For the seven years the Explorer lived with them, acting as if he were their mother's husband, he would march them every weekend down to the plaza and start the clock. The clock was what kept them pinned in place for hours longer than they could bear. They had to stay as still as they could, imagining anything that would help them withstand the rounds of the clock's hands, the sun changing its tilt in the sky. The clock was a dog always baring its teeth. They dared not move. And while even more than a decade had lapsed since they stood frozen like this as children, to do it now would take no effort at all. They were experts at pretending, groomed for it from an early age—Rufina seven, Rafa nine.

"If there's enough money for you to leave by Sunday,"

Rufina said, the smell beneath the bed sour from Rafa's breath and unwashed hair, "you have to leave here and agree to stay alive. Pick one of your precious islands: Pico, Caye Caulker, Jicaro. It doesn't matter." She felt herself holding her breath. Islands were Rafa's fantasy material. He liked to brag he'd been to more than recorded in any atlas. There was nothing more intimate than an island—a place to truly feel one's right size, secure. "If there's not enough," she continued, "you can do whatever you want." There was more gold in his eyes than she'd ever noticed. She thought of winged things trapped under glass.

Outside the bedroom door, in the hallway, their dead mother was making a racket, pounding her feet against the door. For Rafa, the dead mother shimmered in and out of his reality. Mainly, he understood her to have taken the form of memory, though there were moments he wasn't sure. He could sense her near—his nose prickling with her perfume, his hand warming as if touching her cheek—and then he couldn't sense her near at all. It was death he felt near him, a kind of lullaby that overtook him. Rufina, on the other hand, had to deal with Rosalinda, who for her was undoubtedly present, still dressed in her funeral best, having emerged from her dark bedroom on the evening of the fortieth day following her burial to convince her children that despite being dead, she was worthy of their complete attention, a crown of mums still fastened to her head, saffron petals sprinkled down the front of her custom-made dress.

Rafa didn't have much to say in response to his sister's goading. In fact, he didn't say anything at all. His eyes were unfocused, his mouth open, bottom lip cracked, breath rhythmic and warm. He nodded. That was all Rufina needed. The nod. A sign.

An agreement was made: they had the weekend.

She shimmied out from under the bed, scraping her chin on the clay tile as she went, cursing her chin, the tile, their dead mother.

"Rosalinda," Rufina screamed at her mother, whose feet were still pounding against the door. "Enough!" Standing, she secured her good hip beneath her. The noise momentarily stopped. Then Rufina reached down, grabbed Rafa by his ankles, and dragged him to the bathroom and into the shower, where she stripped him of his boxers and cranked the faucet. As the water beat her brother, Rufina thought, of course there will be enough money, of course he will leave town. She could see him on his island, pacing the perimeter of shore. This would mean one less dead; this would mean everything.

The sunburned tourists encircling the brother-sister duo stare. Her arms, her hands, her fingers—Rufina casts a kind of hypnosis with the way she moves, only the top half of her flying, her arms stretching up and over, her hands twirling at the wrists, her fingers seeming to flick like spiders scurrying from water. No one notices her cane, propped against the back of Rafa's metal folding chair, which is why we're telling you. It's a bad habit to miss the most obvious signs. She sings of Baby, her deepest cut of love. Which is to say, once there was a baby, a real baby, her baby. And now there is not. In case you have forgotten, we will remind you that the imagination is a powerful force. For example, now, at this very moment, the tourists have been put under a spell. They do not realize how few words there are in Rufina's songs, how she repeats them. Again, the same phrase, "Oh, my baby, return," and yet, it means something different each time. They want more.

The tourists have driven further than an hour from the nearest airport. Passed sage, piñon, and juniper, mesas, arroyos, and wild horses detailed in this vast southwestern expanse. They have yielded to the narrowing road as it climbs toward Ciudad de Tres Hermanas and then beyond to the hills, toward the mountains, the air thinning as the altitude increases. The enchantment had been activated before they'd even reached the plaza.

Notice how Rufina catches Rafa's eye and directs his gaze to a husband and wife. There is the husband's modest watch and the dimple in his chin, his ironed T-shirt, the crease down the top of each shoulder. There are the wife's neat gold hoops and the ends of her hair turned

under, her small padded bra visible from beneath her
beige linen tank top. Rufina wants them to pay, which
means she'll have to cast a stronger spell. Or Rafa will
have to slyly intervene when the couple starts to argue
about how many bills to surrender to the collection basket. He'll have to think about what he can do. He'll need
to orient himself toward action. He might have to steal
it. Could he steal it? The Explorer taught them this skill,
too, on slow days, how to make sure on the walk home
through the crowded plaza that wallets were slipped
from back pockets and purses were slipped from shoulders with no fuss at all. In Rafa's mind, these thoughts
are buried under wet sand. His head is not something
attached to his body but rather orbiting his body. This
whole scene he's in now could be taking place in a tin can
rusting in an arroyo fifty miles away. Which is to say, he's
barely here. This is a man whose soul has already begun
to unhinge itself. You know what this means.

Rufina sings again, "Come to me. Oh, my baby. Return."
And throws her good hip in the husband's direction. If
the crows watching could reward her for her earnest seduction, they would.

"Why is he playing a guitar with no strings?" the husband asks his wife as she gobbles chili-dusted pistachios
from a paper cone.

Rafa's face is pensive. He's missing two teeth, top front and the one just below. If you see him half-naked—as he appears to the tourists, with no shoes, face hidden by a woven grass hat, the brim lined with mangy feathers, his limbs lean and dark—you'd think to hide your daughters. To look at him, you wouldn't know all the countries he's traveled to during the past nine years, the whole of his twenties. You wouldn't know which languages he's translated, which NGOs have cut him a check. You wouldn't know that six months ago, in the Cala di Volpe, near Montevideo, he gripped the waist of his beloved as he towed him across the fourth-floor hallway, the diamond-patterned carpet reeking of gardenias and dank hide. Rafa had begged not to be left. To be left, his greatest fear. Then the struggle, two men pulling and pushing. Rafa and his beloved. It ended with a hasty kick to Rafa's mouth. The casualties, two of his teeth. And his heart, of course.

"Can't you hear it?" the wife says to her husband. She watches Rafa's pretend playing. "It's part of the charm."

The husband shakes his head. He has failed another test. They are both desperate because theirs is the kind of marriage that grinds a pair down until they are miserable, but miserable together. They are stubborn. Their reward, many more years of shared misery. Don't be mistaken. There are a variety of marriages and you know what they are. The kind you could tolerate and the kind that will eat you from the inside out. No need to lose heart, not yet. But this husband, this wife, these two are particularly awful in the way they choose to show love.

"Use your imagination," the wife offers. She doesn't mean to sound cruel, but it has become her normal voice. Even when she hears it, she's startled. It's her mother's voice and her grandmother's voice when they grew impatient with their own husbands. The voice of a woman who believes she has only one choice—to be yoked to a man who will never fully see her.

"I still don't," the husband says. He's always the last to realize how cruel his wife is to him. This saves him from being embarrassed in front of in-laws, friends, and, when in public, attentive strangers.

The wife ignores him. Another coping mechanism. She licks chili from her fingertips, motions for him to hand her the complementary water bottle from the hotel, which he's stored in the back cargo pocket of his short pants, or "long shorts" as he prefers to call them. Because long shorts to the husband means out of the box, means flexible, and carefree. They remind him of the men he saw in Hawaii on their last vacation. He felt a kinship with those men. Or rather some very young, very faraway part of himself felt a kinship with those men and their attire. The long shorts. He can almost picture himself being mistaken for one of them. An independent man. This is how out of touch with reality he is. This is how severe his longing.

It is the third day of the couple's five-day vacation. We could say they come from the Midwest or the Northwest or the South. We could say his name is John or George or Scott, that her name is Suzie or Tammy or Mary. Tomorrow it will be another couple, the day after, yet another. Under their T-shirts and short pants, where the sun has not scalded them, they are pale with a slight cast, like yogurt gone sour. They are people who cannot really see themselves.

Decades ago, the husband had visited this place or someplace like it. He'd been on a road trip during college break. It was his second year or third year—he can't remember. He wants to remember very badly, but it won't come to him. He could make it up, but that would feel like cheating. He refrains from making up facts. He's not fond of cheaters. The wife has never been, or visited once when she was in kindergarten. Some state in the Southwest, some miniature city, mountains all around. In the days leading up to their departure, the expanse of the state on the map had made her eyes blur. She had stared at it endlessly.

The wife had chosen Ciudad de Tres Hermanas because it kept appearing in the travel magazines—*Condé Nast Traveler, Travel + Leisure, National Geographic*—at her allergist's office where she went for her weekly shots. Always, the City of Three Sisters was referred to as a place of magic, conveniently accessible sans passport:

the sky, the light, the mountains, history fused with the present day, a celebration of diverse cultures, living Natives. They had come because it was her idea. Her idea meant no legwork for him. In fact, he'd be cleared from any work at all. They are different when they travel, and they are also the same as they have always been and ever will be. For example, right now, adobe storefronts surround them while historical markers shout older than old, shout Spanish crown, shout holy cross that maims, shout memories of the Wild West—portáls, dirt roads, and bullets the size of men's fingers lodged deep in the earth, pointing. Quite the dramatic backdrop, and yet: same, same. Remember that it's not the miles that will change you, but what you leave behind, if you choose to leave anything behind at all.

"But *she* is unusual, isn't she?" the husband says to his wife, nodding toward Rufina. A dumb smile reshapes his mouth. He takes his first steps toward her. Off again with his faulty connection to reality, with all of his longing.

Two

Propped against the Five & Dime as if she cannot stand up on her own is the angel. You'll notice she is much too tall for a woman. She is fully aware of this and you should be, too. No need to act otherwise. The tourists take note and approach her. They think her another strange sight. A performer in search of her stage, perhaps, definitely worthy of putting on the list and checking off. Cameras extend for selfies. She's always out of focus in the shots: grinning with half of her face, her hair a tornado of divine knots and curls, wings tucked out of sight.

The angel studies Rafa and Rufina. She sees them as children again, positioned under the same cottonwood, the basket begging at their feet, the Explorer hovering behind the crowd, preparing his critique, and yet, it's not like that at all. The Explorer is long gone and the mother is, well, you know how mothers can hover, despite distance, despite death.

The angel hums along to Rufina's song. She smokes a cherry Colt, thin and dark as a wet branch. Its cherry cigar flavor nothing close to natural. There is what the angel will say and what the angel will not say. Pay attention to this.

She studies her watch, so many ways to construct time. An hour equals what, exactly? A minute opens even more possibilities—and a second? Barely noticeable, and yet, so delicate, so durable. It all matters, but not in the way you think. There are some things not meant for your intellect, but rather meant for the wild you have forgotten inside you that senses all things. Never mind the watch on the angel's wrist, its plastic face the size of a pebble, the digital numbers lit up:

5:12 pm
Fri. 5.29

Time does not step, moment by moment, into the future. Rather, it twirls in an all-encompassing, multidirectional way, not unlike a nest of roots, which truly seems incomprehensible to those accustomed to noticing only the obvious. You do not have to understand this in order for it to be true. The angel has never attempted an explanation, but here is this weekend, the gamble of it. Here are these two lives.

Three

◇

Rafa nods at the wife in time with the music, or, rather the absence of it. All the *baby*s and all the *holy*s chasing each other in one unending refrain. The nodding helps him feel his head on his body. He has a body. It sits in a chair. His legs are crossed. The guitar on his lap like the tomb of some small creature forced to die before it was ready. In this way, his nodding, his body, pins him to this actual moment, not some moment imagined or remembered, but this very instant. Something inside him is still interested in living; notice how much this interest irritates him.

The wife, realizing that Rafa's attention has spotlighted her, laughs. She lowers her chin as if readying herself for a photograph. Her most flattering pose—tip of nose pointed down, right cheek forward, palms mounted on hips. If she could shimmy her shoulders, she would. In her mind, she can dance, is dancing. It's her body that doesn't pick up the signal. Instead, she lifts her elbows, continues to laugh—a hesitant, awkward noise. Bless her heart. There just might be a pinch of rebellion inside her. You'll notice she resembles a hen. Careful, all she needs is someone to believe in her.

Rafa strums the absence of guitar strings. Squints. His nodding continues, steady. It could mean anything. Less than twenty-four hours ago, he had been tucked beneath his mother's bed, where he watched a clutter of dust hanging precariously from the web of a spider. His lower back locked in spasm. He could still smell his mother. Rufina was sidling up next to him, cursing. The wife squirms because she thinks it's about her, his gaze. Her cheeks flush. She is almost dancing, so close, and yet.

It's not the wife that has Rafa's attention, it's her shadow, the shape of it, the subtle shifts in gradation. Don't be confused, this has nothing to do with the placement of the sun—that flaming beast plowing its way across the sky—but has everything to do with the wife's internal ratio of darkness and light. Her shadow, a committed subject, both her and not her, cast flat onto the ground, destined to doggedly follow her through her days. All that she refuses to acknowledge is perceptible

by those who have the gift to see inner shadows exter-
nally displayed. We could easily say not many possess
this gift. Rafa measures how dense the darkness is. And
there, swimming beneath the blackened surface, an image barely visible. He's seen it before. Not an unusual
arrangement for a woman like this: queen with a goat.
As Rafa studies the image, it becomes clear she is sitting high in a tree, on a sturdy limb. It's drizzling. The
goat is tethered to a rope leash tied to the trunk. Know
this: Rosalinda would note not only the quality of darkness in the shadow but the image itself. She would have
been able to decipher whether this queen had children
or grandchildren and how many. Would have discerned
the ridges of her deepest wounds, detailed her symbol of
royalty—crown, scepter, sword studded with jewels, and
if so, which jewels. If her hair were braided, the style of
braid, what the expression was on her face. Rosalinda had
seen the potential in her son and tried to help him hone
his ability, but it was as if certain obvious details would
always stay hidden from him. Due to his own stubbornness, she'd figured. Rafa slows his scan, sees an inverted
crown under the hind end of the goat. His mother had
the power to translate and apply the meaning of these
symbols in relationship to the person being studied.
Which is to say, she'd end her observations by asking
one question. That one question was a kind of medicine,
a drawing salve of sorts. A way to incite attention, clarity,

and the cure—transformation. Rafa has never been able to see that clearly, or interpret the meaning successfully. Never once has he been able to formulate the question that could lead to understanding and to action. In spite of this, when he looks at people, he cannot help but see what is following them, the dark matter of their silhouettes. How desperate it is to be included.

The husband, several feet ahead of his wife, has inched closer and closer to Rufina, who is planted in front of the only speaker, dented and duct-taped, merely a prop. The cord of the microphone slithers between her grip and its insertion point at the speaker when not anchored to its stand. On top of the speaker squats the collection basket. The husband's head bobs, not unlike a goose strutting toward the edge of water. And like a goose, he leans his head forward as if preparing for the imminent strike.

Rufina's blouse grips her breasts. It's all it can do to keep them contained. The strained stitching travels in tiny purple threads that dot the seams and cinch her, a corset of sorts. A row of shy, petite pearl buttons trace her midline. Some are missing and some still manage to hang on. Her hair sighs loose, a net of it, waiting.

"My baby," she sings. Her voice saturates the crowd.

Unlike her brother, Rufina wears shoes—wooden heels, buckskin laces—a skirt that could gather the world. Her brother's ankles dangle from the bottoms of his pin-striped navy trousers. She glances at them while she sings, thinks them a crude pair of crossbones. He wears a matching pin-striped vest without a shirt. Instead of fixing his teeth, he spent his money on ink, evidence of love attempted, love failed. A green mess of tattoo covers his heart in Sanskrit. Ask him what the symbol means and he'll say, "Keep Out." Or whatever else he feels like making it mean.

"Holy. Holy." The notes are getting higher and more pitchy. She's holding them for longer with each breath, more of a siren than a voice meant to please.

Unlike her brother's, Rufina's skin is blanched. They have different fathers after all, which makes them half-siblings, half-strangers. Each of them a souvenir from an intimate war. Rafa is older by twenty months, born during harvesttime. Rufina was born during planting season. For him, winter is always on the verge—slow, deep, hidden. For her, perpetual spring—shedding, expansive, fresh. He stinks of peat, cumin, and fresh piñon sap. She stinks of peat, cumin, and fresh piñon sap.

"Return." Rufina releases all of her breath into this last note. It rings out, piercing the ears of every living thing for miles. Listen closely and you can hear it, too.

Four

◆

Officer Armijo watches from the newspaper vending boxes on the corner. He sees the back of Rufina. The way the hem of her skirt is shorter on the right. The way her spine curves ever so slightly in the wrong direction. Her hips, a mismatched pair. It's clear to him some internal part of her is protesting. He's trained himself to track such things. He wants to guide her, lead her to be the woman he knows her to be, a woman who can grow a new heart no matter how severe the previous damage, a woman who can remember the force of her own two feet on the ground. As he watches her, he dreams of ripe fruit—apples and peaches—that at this very moment are ever so slowly swelling and sweetening. He dreams of the sound water makes in the acequia at night. His job is to keep the peace. Depending on the day, and the situation he finds himself in, he has an entirely different idea about what this means. He knows men, hidden in the night, snort and stomp the ground; women feel the thick, wet potential inside themselves, pulsing. It may or may not incite violence. It's late spring, after all, and the moon is waxing. None of this is in his control.

Laborers cross the plaza on their way to the bank, where they wire money to husbands, wives, or parents thousands of miles away. We could say they come from Honduras or Guatemala or Mexico. Look closer, see the blisters on toes from borrowed shoes, see the burn marks on fingers from scalding dishes, see the relief and the burden of being free. They leave the bank penniless again and cross the plaza on the way to a second or third shift.

The Original Enduring Ones positioned on the portál of the government building are ever watchful. Rafa had named them years ago. He had wanted to protect them from what the Explorer had called them: savage, squaw, injun, chief. Clearly, they bothered the Explorer when they were on the plaza, at the grocery store and the gas station, in the laundromat. He resented their presence. As vendors, they were competition and meant less income from the tourists. "Bad artists, lazy, drunks." It was all said lightly as the Explorer raised his left eyebrow. As if he dared someone to correct him, always ready to turn the slur into a joke. He didn't really mean it. Wasn't it funny, after all? These silly names. These silly people. He'd imitate their creativity in a second if it meant attention, he'd tell their stories, too. Even when he managed to call them Indians and Native Americans, it sounded degrading. As in "I can be a better Indian than they could ever be," his far-off gaze locked in fantasy. But Rafa had stared at them all those hours he posed as the Explorer's mannequin and saw what he felt was their humanness. The sight of them reminded him to breathe while he stood immobile, as if a cast poured by the Explorer's hands. They saw him, too, and it came to him one long day in the direct sun, "The Original Enduring Ones." It seemed obvious to him, the need to show respect, as with anyone. It was what he himself craved. Whenever the Explorer would hear Rafa's term, he'd say, "Well, aren't you clever?" The ends of his mouth bent into something related to disgust.

Now, look the way Rafa looked at them all those years ago and still does. Note their attention to the seen and the unseen. Which is to say, there are those who have always been here, their DNA sung into the rocks. It's quite possible that, while Rafa understood this as a boy, you will not. Notice how they are positioned behind their silver, turquoise, and coral-beaded strands of sellables, their black and mica pots, their bank bags unzipped and ready to make change. Leaning against truck hoods with braids, buzz cuts, or hair bound at the napes of their necks, speaking Diné, or Keres, or Tewa. Languages that unlock a reality, parallel to yours. Take, for example, when the raven calls from the cottonwoods, and you hear *caw, caw*, but the Diné woman at the stand selling mutton fajitas hears *caution, caution* and steps out of the line just as a homeless man crashes into her stand, splashing hot grease onto the sidewalk where moments before she had been standing. Not all is equally seen and heard. Just as the land knows, the Original Enduring Ones know that this, too, shall pass. After all, it's been thousands of years.

Officer Armijo waits ten yards away from Rufina's side. If he asks them for a permit, he knows what will happen. Rufina will say, "Stop bothering us, Lucio." She will give him her back. Rafa will say, "You're gonna have to try harder than that." He will look Lucio up and down, chew the inside of his cheek, waiting for a comeback, the hook. It will be as if the three of them are in high school all over again. Ninth grade, homeroom, Ms. Abeyta. In the back row, Lucio inching his desk closer to Rufina's, his backpack weighted with another offering. Biscochitos he helped his mother bake, the tops crusted with cinnamon sugar and a handful of cherries from the tree outside his bedroom window—the same tree that had been calling to him since he was a toddler, its branches insistent against the glass. He wanted to tell Rufina that each sweet orb of fruit was an entire blushing planet, waiting to be discovered by her mouth, but he disclosed no such thing. And when the bell rang, in the hallway Rafa was waiting for her, the two merging as they traversed the territory of the school. Rafa sulking, distracted. Rufina striding crisp and purposeful and straight. And that's how the school days went, Lucio positioning himself at the door of her next class, Lucio loitering in the lunchroom by the trash cans, Lucio lingering after the last bell. It was everything he could do to be close to Rufina.

The tourists' large white heads bob and their necks blister in the sun's unrelenting grasp. Saucers of sweat stains under their armpits, asses pressed flat from sitting on the plane, from sitting on the shuttle, from sitting in the hotel, in the restaurants, in the bicycle taxis. Sitting at the job that made this trip possible. Sitting is what they do. They have mastered sitting. Their legs, those unsightly stubs and sticks of purpose, are punctuated by highly functional rubber sandals. They are necessary guests, and yet, see how easy it is to resent them, to see all tourists as one tourist? Just as easy as it is for the tourist to see a price tag dangling from every visible thing, including from the wrist of every indiscernible brown arm.

Officer Armijo's fingers trace his badge, his gun, his collar. It's a tic he's developed in the twelve years he's been an officer. A way to convince himself of the obvious—*he is in control.* He rests his hands on the disobedient mound of his belly.

The duo. Brother, sister.

Exotic, the husband thinks as if he's naming her, adjusting the belt of his long shorts.

Exotic, the wife thinks as if she's naming him, her hands cupping her elbows, swaying from side to side.

Rufina wants the husband near her. Then, she will reach out and trail her hands down the tops of his arms. She knows this has the power to make him shiver, twitch his head as if trying to rid water trapped in one of his ears.

If Rufina wants them to pay, they will pay. She starts the business with her mouth. She can mimic a trumpet, she can whistle, howl, and wail, trill as if an entire band unto herself. It's the whistling—the sweet, sexy surprise of it—that undoes the husband. Baits him.

He grabs Rufina around the waist, pretending that he can dance her. His grip is animal, his smile frozen. She can feel him stiff against her. Step to the side. Step to the other side. Forward. Back. Forward. She is without her cane and her left hip drags noticeably behind, missing the beat. As the husband steps again, his leg advances too far, knocking over the microphone stand, which crashes against the pavement, echoing throughout the plaza. The Original Enduring Ones turn their heads. Front-row seats for hundreds of years. None of this surprises them.

Rafa is close behind, as if he could protect her, as if she belongs to him. Rufina spits one word into his ear. *Wallet.* It's a suggestion that makes him almost come to life.

"What are you doing?" the wife shouts to her husband; her voice carries voltage.

The husband spins around on his heels. He's lost his way.

The tourists cannot see the impending crime, the husband and wife's confusion, the brother and sister's scheme. They are blinded by papel picado as it ruffles in a sigh of wind, ice of all flavors is scooped into disposable cups, candy wrappers flit down the gutters. The tourists see the sky, bricks made of dirt, straw, and spit. They see silver and turquoise.

The husband's head is sweating, beads of it rolling through the desperate remaining strands of hair, down the front of his ordinary face. "Just going along," he says, "with the song." He wipes his palms against the front of his thighs. All that holy, all that returning. He tucks his shirt in, straightens up, glances sheepishly around the plaza.

This is the moment Officer Armijo steps forward. He asks to see Rufina's permit to perform on the plaza.

The husband and wife linger. The wife puts her hands

in her pockets. The husband puts his hands on the back of his neck. They continue to shift and twitch. Their hands finally hang at their sides. She reaches for him. They lock their fingers together.

Officer Armijo picks up the mic and stand. The mic is crushed. The stand bent. He offers it to Rufina. She reaches instead for the spine of her cane. It's her left leg that's frozen, the right leg strong enough to hold her up—her brother, too.

The wife says, "At least let us pay you for the damage." She spins her wedding band. It has always been too loose.

The husband reaches for his wallet. His hands pull at all the cargo pocket possibilities. He does this multiple times, says, "That's strange." Says, "It was right here." Says to the wife, "You must have it."

The wife is not carrying her purse. Still, she pats herself down. Makes a show of it. She produces a nickel, a penny, a one-dollar bill.

Both of their faces flush. The wife's narrow nostrils flare. The husband pulls on his earlobe. Their eyes flit to each other and to the ground. Then, the wife says to Rufina, "Will you be here tomorrow? We'll come tomorrow. We want to pay you."

Rufina's eyes tell Rafa things no one else can decipher. She nods her head at the wife.

"We want to pay you," the husband echoes. He reaches out to touch Rufina, a gesture meant to comfort.

His hand hovers at her wrist, then her shoulder, then the top of her head, but never makes contact. He settles both hands behind his back, one trapping the other.

"Well, technically," Officer Armijo says, "if you don't have a permit, you can't accept money."

"You don't have anyone else to bother, Lucio?" Rufina says. "No wives trying to slit their husbands' throats, no heroin overdoses, no neglected elders, no drunks crossing the center line on Highway Fourteen?" She rests on the cane, anchored in front of her pelvis, her whole body tilted to the right. There is roughly fifty dollars in the basket, which she has covered with a scarf. She signals to her brother, who gathers the damaged equipment and stuffs it all into the little red wagon they use to haul their props. "Let's rename it," Rufina had said earlier in the day as they'd walked into town. They took the path through the woods, along the narrow, deep vein of river that flowed into, through, and out of town. The wagon had belonged to the mother and had been christened Cacahuate, long ago. "We're not renaming anything," Rafa had said in return.

"Lucio," Rufina says. "Get out of our way."

Rufina remembers the last time Lucio delivered Rosalinda home, another offense of public indecency. A misunderstood woman who had suffered enough in her life, whose daughter he'd wanted to protect and couldn't. Now look what he'd become, an adult with a badge and a car with sirens and lights, acting as Rosalinda's chaperone. How patient he was as he led her from the front seat of his cruiser to the door. One of his arms around her waist, another holding her hand, as gracefully as if he were dancing her. He'd made her smile. She'd made him stop every time she had something to say. It had taken nearly fifteen minutes to travel the length of the yard. From the window above the kitchen sink, Rufina had full view of the father in Lucio. It detonated something inside her, causing a wreck her thoughts could not sort through.

The wallet Rafa had slipped into his vest pocket bulges, but he conceals it with the inside of his forearm. On his wrist, the silver bracelet his mother had given him when he turned sixteen—not unlike a handcuff. As he drags the little red wagon, its floppy wheels chatter incessantly. He had pulled their sick mother around the garden in it, sang along to the records playing inside the house, tried to make her laugh with crude confessions he'd never imagine telling another. Lovers on psychedelics, all the begging, the scratches, the temporary courage, the wicked pleading and role-playing. The way in which he could figure-eight his hips. All the voices he could mimic. Never mind. Remembering makes it more difficult.

Officer Armijo stops the wagon with his boot.

"What do you want now?" Rafa asks. He drops the handle of the wagon, positions his arms across his torso in a way that keeps the wallet hidden.

"If it's just for the one day," Officer Armijo says, "I'll let it go." His fingers trace badge, gun, collar. "It's just for the one day, right?" He is in control. "I'm not going to see you here tomorrow with no permit, right?"

Rufina pivots and throws her hip forward. She grabs the wagon's handle and taps her brother's thigh with her cane, as if he were a horse and had just been instructed to get moving. Her gait makes its own song.

"Right?" Officer Armijo repeats, standing alone. The plaza has begun to drain of life. Vendors wrapping and packing, trunks of cars stuffed, tourists stroll out the side streets spoking in all four cardinal directions.

Along the periphery, the Original Enduring Ones chatter with one another. Laughter sparks. They measure the sun against the times on their watches, discuss the consequence of being cast in the wrong role, how many generations has it been now? The chief, the medicine man, the drunk, the silent soldier who always dies. How many generations has it been now? They laugh some more. Who wants to be the leading man? The everyday guy? Deep in the rocks, their songs flicker.

✦

In the patrol car, Officer Lucio Armijo delays starting the engine. He shakes the keys in his palm as if they were dice, stares at the pattern of crow shit on his windshield, remembers the way Rufina's chest bloomed with each breath, accentuated by the curve of her pose, the deep crease between her breasts. The tight curls of hair caught against her neck, the string of embroidery hanging loose at her shoulder. He knows that when he sits down to eat dinner with his wife and four sons, each time he swallows, he'll see the shape of her lips, the tiny row of buttons down her front—a tender gauntlet—the button above her navel missing. And when he sleeps, he'll dream of feeling all this against his fingertips.

Five

Before Rufina had spotted her brother under their mother's bed, and forced him to bet his life, there had been a week of hide-and-seek in the house—Rufina locating stashes of Rosalinda's pain pills, hiding them, finding more. Rafa trailing her in an attempt to track the collection he'd amassed. While Rafa had banished himself to the space beneath his mother's bed, Rosalinda sat on the floor in the hallway, her back against the door. Rufina had to step over her. Each time she did, she'd strike her mother's shins with her cane. The mother ignored her daughter as the mother had a habit of doing. This, of course, made Rufina strike her harder and more often.

"Is this what you want for him?" Rufina asked. "To make him suffer more than you did when you were alive?

Four months? Enough. Be dead already." Notice what Rufina did not say: "I hate you for leaving me."

Every morning since her mother's ghostly resurrection, when Rufina woke, she willed it to be the day her mother was still alive. Instead, there was the mournful mother pulling at the hooks of distress lodged deep in her mournful son. Dead, not dead.

"It always has to be about you," Rufina said. Notice she did not say to her mother, "I still need you."

"What do you know?" Rosalinda said, finally giving in to Rufina's pestering. Her hair was chopped unevenly above her shoulders. That was Rufina's fault. "You have no idea what this is about. Besides, you have your distractions—the earnest cop, Baby, and your other stupid fantasies." *Stupid fantasies* being code for the Explorer—Rufina's grieving for him after he'd left, her commitment to imagining his return. How many years had it been now—the age her child should be, nearly fifteen. She resisted the number, a sharp fact she would bend and remake into whatever she found most comforting—three weeks, six months.

"You still haven't—" Rufina stopped, she was aiming for an insult, but lost her fire. This was not uncommon for Rufina, to lose her words with her mother when she needed them as ammunition the most. What was it Rufina was going to say? "You still haven't forgiven me"? Or was it "You still don't love me like you love him"?

Of course Rosalinda wasn't concerned with Rufina. Or rather, it was her son she was concerned with and there wasn't anything left for her daughter. Rufina wanted to protect Rafa, but couldn't find the words that would ward the mother off. Trigger a phrase that would inflict hurt, cause the mother to recoil. Clearly, Rosalinda did not hesitate before attacking, and won every round.

Rosalinda wore her signature dress, one of the Explorer's designs, custom made for her petite figure. Vertical ruffles ran down her, severe and crisp as fins. The neckline plunged in the front as well as the back. Around her shoulders, a huipil, woven blue, purple, and green. Bracelets of assorted widths and metals stacked up and down both of her forearms, thick carved bands, stones larger than her knuckles piled onto her fingers, medallions for earrings hung down past her collarbones. Her neck was bare. There was the mole in the cup of her throat Rufina and Rafa would fight over. They each wanted to name it, to possess that tiny patch of skin. A bundle of pink and red sword lilies concealed her legs. Blush streaked each one of her cheeks. Her lips hid under an attack of fuchsia. The yellow-and-orange headdress of mums made her appear larger; however, even in death, she was out of place, a refugee.

"What are you planning?" Rufina said. She would not cry in front of her mother. Instead, she bit the tip of her thumb. Grief was a powerful admission and she wasn't having it. Notice she did not say, "Will I ever have you to myself?"

"It doesn't concern you," the mother said. She reached up and put her hand on the doorknob.

Rufina leaned against the wall, letting her grip on the cane relax. "It won't work, will it?" she said. Rufina had been watching her mother, the way she moved around the house—when she lingered in a room, when she escaped into the next—and realized her mother could not come and go as she pleased. If a door had been left open, she could drift in or out, otherwise, she had to wait. Rufina found herself sweeping the mother from the thresholds of entryways with a broom meant for dead leaves and mice. She refused to open any doors. The more the mother wanted to comfort herself with Rafa, the more Rufina kept him away from her. They were nearly inseparable when she was alive—his fingers brushing and braiding her hair, the endless cups of tea made to her exact liking before she'd even asked for them, the way he listened intently to whatever language came out of her mouth, and when she seemed to wilt, his dramatic comedy-infused performance that would lift her. While he traveled, there were the constant phone calls as if he were as close as the next room. Rufina wanted her turn. It was her turn.

Rosalinda twisted her face as if she were going to spit at Rufina. This was not uncommon. While she never spat at her daughter, she would spit in front of her as if to spoil the space where Rufina were about to step. Instead, she grabbed her daughter's cane, put it behind her back, rolled it under her hips so that she was sitting on it.

"You can manage without," the mother said. "Let me see you try."

Rufina considered how to move her mother in order to retrieve her cane. She imagined picking her mother up by her neck. Surely it couldn't cause harm.

"You act like you're in pain," the mother continued. "You don't have any idea what pain is."

"It wasn't my fault," Rufina said. They were talking about the Explorer now. "It wasn't my fault." Which is to say the Explorer had devastated them both, but Rufina was only a girl and Rosalinda was the woman he called *wife*, as if it were a pet name. Know this: dual, simultaneous pregnancies out of which nothing survives carve a particular kind of scar. See the evidence of Rufina's hip. See the way in which she holds on to Baby.

"It's been long enough," the mother said. She wouldn't look at Rufina when the Explorer's memory threatened to resurface. It was a passive punishment, but relentless. Disappearing a daughter by not giving her any attention. She puckered her lips as if there were a cigarette between them, and, keeping her eyes fixed to her lap, said, "Please." The sound of it was worthless, nearly inaudible. She offered a lily stem to Rufina. Held it above her head as if it were a flag of surrender.

"It wasn't my fault," Rufina said, biting her thumb even harder. Notice Rufina doesn't say, "How was I supposed to know what to do?"

Inside the mother's bedroom, Rafa was a collection of scraps beneath the sheets. The palo santo, the copal, the musk of the mother's unwashed scalp, the pungent bittersweet from under her arms still lingering after her death, all of this he used to comfort himself. Why didn't Rufina understand? When the mother left, she took with her his place in the world, which means he had become a dislocated man.

"I'm not letting you in," Rufina said to the mother. "We can't go on like this." The stem of the sword lily was wet. There was no good way to hold it.

The angel had been sitting cross-legged on the couch. She could not see what was happening in the hallway, and yet, she knew very well what was happening. She'd heard everything. The presence of the dead meant the presence of the angel. One followed the other in some unwritten code of grace. "No," she commanded. Her voice carried down the hall. It caught in Rufina's ears. Rufina let go of the flower. The mother swiveled around, placed her heels against the door, and beat on it with her feet. Started to wail. No longer gripping her daughter's cane, Rufina retrieved it. Held it up by her right shoulder as if it were a baseball bat and thwacked her mother's back—to no response, of course.

Meanwhile, Rafa was naked under the sheets. He couldn't remember how long he had been sprawled there. There were many things he couldn't remember: airports, taxis, paychecks, drinks with colleagues, another man's mouth. The mother's candles continued to burn. Votives cluttered the surface of the nightstand, lined the mantle above the kiva fireplace, the windowsills. He lit her cigarettes, but did not smoke them. The butts stood in teacups filled with sand, along with the incense, burning from top to bottom. An entire carton of cigarettes was still under her bed. Occasionally, he'd hear Rufina put on a record. Something the Explorer had left, something the mother had not broken. Something with hand drums and tambourines, horns and incessant high notes.

A memory played against the screen of his mind. Was he nine? Ten? His mother would send him down the hill to the liquor store for a pack of cigarettes, but this particular day when he was especially lonely for her, instead of buying her a pack as usual, he'd bought her a single cigarette. He'd ridden back with it unlit in his mouth and delivered it to her, along with a single match. He'd struck the match against a loose brick on the portál and cupped his hand around her lips. This had been how the Explorer had done it. Rafa had been watching the ways in which the Explorer had treated his mother closely. The way he'd pulled her to him, or pushed her away. His hands had been larger than her face and were often relocating her in space as if she were a figurine—from the floor to the counter, the stool to the couch, from the bed to the top of the dresser. Rafa rounded his fingers near the flame, his pinky resting on her upper lip. Her eyes did not leave his for the duration of this gesture. Then he sat on the cement before her, inhaling, while she sat in her little wooden Sunday school chair, exhaling. Twenty minutes later when she wanted another, down the hill he went, pedaling as fast as he could. She had to wait for him, of course. She was dependent on him, which is to say he knew this, and due to this fact, felt himself on his way to becoming a man.

This continued for the entire day. One cigarette, one match, the gesture, the lingering. The need, the quest, the delivery. The Explorer observed from his post in the kitchen, but did not say a word. Rufina sat in the rocking chair on the roof waiting for her mother to join her, as Rosalinda occasionally did when she grew tired of painting on the floor. Instead, Rosalinda's creative rhythm was disturbed with unnecessary waiting. The Explorer watched her face flatten, knew what was soon to come, but did not warn the boy. She had to take longer breaks from her ink portraits. Black on her thumbs, on the heels of her palms, the glistening wet portraits, the pleading conveyed in the eyes of her subjects, as if trapped. Even Rufina, from above, could hear her mother's grunts of impatience as if she were a dog that'd gone too long without being fed. It was the summer, dry heat, and every day was endless. The dragonflies flew in swarms that year. Later that summer, the couple from Chile would arrive. For decades, season after season, Rafa and Rufina would still carry this summer with them and the impact the couple had made.

When, on a return trip, the unlit cigarette fell from Rafa's mouth and broke in half, he was curious what his mother would do. Should he go back for another and be more careful? Or would this give them more time together, offering her half a cigarette at a time? He decided it would in fact give them more time. He was convinced of this when he presented it to her. Instead of letting him put a match to what was left of it, his mother strode into the kitchen. When she returned, she had a paring knife. She used it to stab the front tire on his bicycle. "I've had enough of you," she'd told him, and slammed the front door.

He had to walk, but he came back with two packs, which he laid on her nightstand. In the time he'd been gone, she'd crawled into bed and had turned herself completely toward the wall. The incense smoke curled, the candlelight snapped. She whispered in that language none of them understood. The Explorer had thought it all hilarious and, when Rafa came in, sulking, he had laughed from the sink where he was peeling beets. Rufina continued rocking, alone, on the roof.

The mother waited until the next morning to draw her son into her chest, bury him in her hair, kissing the dried sweat on his delicate neck, front and back. She had been thorough. Her fresh lipstick, orange and sticky, marked him like the tracks of a tiny, temperamental bird.

Throughout his adulthood, each time he returned to the house and to the mother, it was as if he were stepping into a hole, the dark and familiar cavern of Rosalinda, who would submerge him, then consume him. Which is to say, this was how he came to understand love, this love that he longed for, then resisted when it came.

He had been trained throughout his life to wait for his mother to summon him from Mumbai, Rome, Beirut, D.C., Geneva. Then: her hair around him, her laughing, his face covered with her lips, the tracks of that rare bird on him, the son. The only son.

She was wailing in the hallway. Is that what he heard? The sound of her feet thundering against the door outpaced his heart.

Mi hijo. Mi amor. Mi conejito.

Rafa stared at the miniature candle flames twitching inside the votive glasses. He thought of her most often-told story, her legendary escape, the long migration, the fantastical journey of it. She told him how she could feel him growing inside her like a vine as she crawled along cactus-studded paths at night, stones splitting her knees. Every time she told it, the details changed—what were the borderlands, how many family members were killed, four or fifteen; how long it took, three weeks or six months; who was chasing her, rebels or military; if there was help or not along the way; whether it was women or men or children that offered her food, or was it the guanaco, chinchilla, or capybara that told her which way to go. And then there were the details that remained the same—she had no choice but to run from her village: there was gunfire and smoke; the volcano was at her back; she had become pregnant and thought the spirits of the dead were hiding inside her, growing in mass.

Even the consistent details of the story seemed as though they were near-truths. All of it overwhelming—memories, lies. Rafa had once attempted to track her route. The impossibility of it. He remembered the mountains, the rivers, deserts, the variety of climates and ecotones, all that space in between. The silence in place of answered questions, no matter how he had phrased the questions. There was the weight of never knowing something so simple as where his mother, his people were from. When his mother had been alive, the mystery could be camouflaged by more fantastical stories. She always had another, more convincing tale at the ready, but now, what was there?

Rufina was at the door. "Rafa," she said above the sound of the mother's kicking. "Raphael!"

In her bed, under the sheets, tucked into himself, he could almost feel her close. Were there any more packs of cigarettes under the bed? He should look. He would crawl down and look.

Rufina tried again, louder. "Unlock the door, Rafa. I've got an idea. Let's use the weekend."

This is how it began, where it took root. And still, Rufina had to wait days before prying open the door, crawling under the bed, and making her brother swear.

While Rafa made his sister wait, he'd willed himself to feel his mother close. Pushed her away. Pulled her close. Pushed. He felt the absence inside himself, the hole within. He spoke the mother's name like a mantra, calling her back to him. Rosalinda, Rosalinda, Rosalinda. His mouth open, empty, bottomless. Searching for her nipple, for her attention to nourish him, to remind him he was still alive, among the living. A man, a boy, an infant.

Six

○

Dusk has begun the slow opening of its cloak as Rafa and Rufina step off the road and onto the path that takes them through the woods, alongside the stream and back home. Being on this path is not being in the city at all. A crease of canyon, it flushes in green overgrowth. Dense canopy of leaves—bush and tree—the path becomes more and more narrow, winding. Walls of trees and bushes force Rafa and Rufina to walk single-file. Hummingbirds flit and a sparrow hawk rustles its kill in the brush. Butterflies perch on hedgehog and cholla cacti. They hear children's voices calling out to each other in laughter but cannot see anyone. Rufina thinks she can smell them. Children emit a particular fragrance, part animal, part blossom, to which she is sensitive. "You're

BROTHER, SISTER, MOTHER, EXPLORER

it!" a voice yells out. More laughter. "I'm always it," another voice responds. Laughter continues. The voices slowly quiet. Trickle out. Rafa thinks they'll come upon the children at any moment. Instead, once they hit the clearing, he sees an empty tire swing, twirling.

At the end of the path, they have to climb a steep incline. Rafa lifts the wagon, carrying it to the top, where the road appears again. As he does so, his toes dig into the dirt.

Rafa and Rufina make their way up the drive, the wagon tilting and jumping across the gravel. Rafa picks it up and sets it under the portál. There is Rosalinda reclining on the diseased couch under the apricot tree with its fresh shoots. Rufina points her cane at Rosalinda, walks past, ducks under the low frame of the back door, closes it behind her. Goes for Baby in her bedroom. Which is to say, she goes for this infant that has been an infant for fourteen years, that has never left the house, and has been seen only by Rafa and Rosalinda. What is Baby if not armor against her mother, armor against being unloved, unnecessary. With Baby in her arms, her focus narrows. While her forehead is against Baby's, she can feel the imagined breath. Because there is Baby, Rufina is a mother, too, loved and needed.

"What took you so long, mi conejito?" the mother asks her son, her hands cupped over her heart. "Come lie down with me," she says. She is no taller than she was at twelve. Her skin two shades darker than either of her children. "Why won't you wear shoes?" she asks her son. "Did I cross countries, rivers, mountains, deserts, beg for my life in order for you to be born, so that you could grow into a man, and not to wear shoes?"

His toenails need attention. He's unwashed. He sags into the couch, as if he'll surrender, then stands back up. He hears the mother. He doesn't hear the mother. He paces the yard, circles the well. He pauses by the compost, looking for worms, for evidence of skunk. Just beneath the soil, energy simmers, the earth is moving, opening, seeds are shape-shifting.

Rafa heads into the house, ducks under the low frame, leaves the door open. He squeezes lemon into water, adds salt and sips while he stares out the narrow, horizontal window stretched above the kitchen counter. The "lookout" window, the Explorer used to call it. As in, no one passing by could go unnoticed. Who needed a guard dog when you had a window like this, he used to say. As if looking out a window were protection. You, of course, know better. Know that seeing happens with more than your eyes.

The Grandmothers to All parade past on bicycles. They ring the bells on their handlebars and wave at the house. This has been their routine for decades. We could say that the Grandmothers to All consist of elderly women who live at a compound farther up the canyon.

They may or may not have ever been married. They may or may not have had their own children. Retired from working as lawyers and professors, genealogists and archivists, hospice specialists and midwives, they now keep a library of seeds and decorate altars with them. They tend to the bees and hundreds of varieties of lavender, which they distill into essences that can heal whatever begs to be healed. Notice they also grow garlic. Once harvested, they braid the leaves, pinning the green plait to archways all over the compound. They're sap collectors as well—the Grandmothers to All—piñon, cottonwood, cedar. Resin mixed with the lavender essences. Which is to say they understand what is cyclical, natural, and sacred. In addition, they rescue women in need. Because aren't women just an extension of the natural world? Just like you? Know this: it was the Grandmothers to All who were waiting at the border nearly thirty years ago with blankets, food, and water for Rosalinda. Two of them lifted her off the ground and carried her into the car. They led her into the house in this canyon where she would birth both her children, raise them, and then, years later, return her body to the earth. Meanwhile the Grandmothers to All were close by, watching.

The mother calls to Rafa from outside, from her couch nest. She is always calling to him. She longs to feel his warm body. He senses something, uncertain. "Lie down with me. Come and lie down."

In the kitchen, he walks in circles around the table. Finds a bottle of hot sauce, squirts it onto his tongue. Pretends he'll squirt it up his nose. Rufina enters, her hair wet, a long T-shirt aiming for her knees, the baby strapped to her back. Her cane ticks the floor like a lazy clock grown tired from keeping time. She has a fresh scratch on her cheek from Baby's nails. It's hot pink and glistening. Baby's eyes are large and seem to swallow everything in the room.

Rufina gives her brother a look. "How old are you, and still acting like you'll shoot it up your nose? Yes, you exist. Pain tells you so." She takes the bottle from him. "Enough."

"Can you hear that?" Rafa asks. He's touching his ears as if Rufina doesn't know what ears are.

"It's nothing," she says, returning the bottle to its rightful place on the top shelf in the fridge. Under her breath she mutters, "Our lady of longing."

"It won't stop."

"Ignore it," Rufina says.

"Is it her? Do you hear it?"

Rufina adjusts Baby's neck, gathers eggs, cracks them into a ceramic bowl, beats them frothy with a three-pronged fork. She aches for their mother more than Rafa could ever comprehend. Rufina's ache is older than her teeth. It cements her neck and back, forms a shield across her entire chest. Keeps her breath shallow.

"Can you see her?" he asks. Rafa snaps his arms, from

the elbows down, as if he could propel himself far away, high above, to someplace else. His arms are a blur. He is three years old again. He is a bird. Which is to say, he thinks he can fly.

Rufina stops frothing the eggs. She watches her brother's undoing. It splits her heart. She acts as if she were the eldest, as if she were the mother, as if she were the surrogate wife. "Enough," she says. "It's the same for me as it is for you."

Rafa's arms melt. He worms his hand into his vest pocket. Pulls out the wallet. He's unsure if he can trust the bet, Rufina's silly game, the timing of the weekend, his intermittent resolve to live.

"Check the wallet," she says.

"This isn't going to work."

"There could already be plenty of money," she says. "We might not have to go back for more." She pulls Baby around to her front, who swats at Rufina's cheek. She tightens the knot on her rebozo, kisses the top of baby's head. "What about our bet?"

The things Rafa has had more of than Rufina—money, stamps in his passport, attention from the mother, lovers—and still, he will always want more. Rufina knows this, knows how competitive he is. And yet, she will always be the one who is stronger.

"I might be winning," she says. At this, Baby stops squirming and grins. A rind of flesh. "Open the wallet."

The slots are crammed with plastic cards. Inside the cash pocket, the sole reason for the bulge: a collection of receipts. Rafa's fingers sift through one and then the other, throwing them to the floor. They flit and arc and twirl as if confetti. Baby watches, rapidly blinking. There is a desperate magic to it.

"Money," she says. "How much?"

He pulls out two bills, a ten and a five.

"Not possible."

"I'm winning," he says.

The iron skillet on the stove begins to smoke. Rufina pours the scrambled yolk. Immediately the air stinks of burnt eggs. A charred film forms on the omelet, dark and rubbery as leather.

"Not fucking possible."

Rosalinda stands at the threshold. She has one foot in. Look at her face. She's about to cry, don't you think? Poor mother, always in need of comfort. The formal bones of her face. Poured from the same stubborn mold of her mother and her mother's mother. A particular kind of face, a brown woman's face, cast from the earth itself. She peels the dress from her body as if clothes were unnatural. There, her slack breasts, the black wire thatch between her legs, a giant tangle. Her feet, flat against the rug, standing there with them. Her body, their home country. Her body, their creation story. Her body, the catalogue of all the relatives they will never know.

"Cook the fish," Rufina says. It's a command meant to distract him. She can see he's spiraling into memory about the mother. He isn't conscious of how close Rosalinda is, but deep within, he's activated. Another wave of memory and grief—crashing.

As Rafa unwraps the fish and splashes oil, all he sees is the mother. She is pocket-sized. Even smaller. He sees her as if through a pinhole in his memory. She is a riddle he was once taught and then forgot. A moment from the past seizes him. He thinks: Was I the one in the bath with her? Or was I the one standing over her? Was I three or sixteen? Was I the one washing her? Or was she washing me? The soap gathering around her thighs. On her knees in the water. Was it winter outside? My mother with her skin, the territory of my mother. My mother in the bath on her knees. The oil of the soap filming the surface. Watching the soap, a brick of white, submerge. The ferocity with which she scrubbed herself, the hair and the mouth, and the tongue and the lips, all of it wet and opening. The kind of dirty that would never come clean. Still, he watched as she scrubbed and the water frothed and grew, the suds tripling in size, white the color of making it better, froth the size of countries, the size of continents. White, the color of tourists, the color of politicians and priests, the color of the Explorer. Water sloshing the sides of the tub as she rinsed and rinsed and rinsed. "No more," she's screaming. He feels nauseated. Which is to say these times he remembers in the bath with his mother are times he has tried to forget. He's never been sure if it was her shame he was feeling or his own. Was he supposed to save her or was she supposed to save him?

The fish is white, too, like the soap, like the water, and slick with oil. The oven door is open. Heat spills out. The pan is before him. He covered the fish with lemon and tin foil. Surely he did this, moments ago, even if he doesn't remember. He stands to the left of the oven door. Walks around to the right. Again, to the left. Heads for the right. Rufina intervenes, grabbing the glass dish and placing it inside. Rafa laughs at himself. There is something just beneath his skin. Rufina sees it, the thing that won't let him rest, that won't let him fully commit to living.

She hands him a jar of olives. He tips it back, drinks the juice. She passes him an avocado and a knife. He sinks the blade, begins to peel.

Rosalinda is now on her hands and knees. She crawls under the table, beneath the cloth draping it. Hides among her children's legs.

Everything in the kitchen is chipped because of Rosalinda. Even when she was alive, she had to assert her own existence with one mess after another. Rufina can't stand the way she moves the dishes at night. Juice glasses, sauce bowls, platters—littering the counter, the living room floor, the bathroom sink. The tink and clank of them against each other, against the stacked rings on Rosalinda's fingers. She nicks them with her clumsy touch, not quite sure of the edges. Edge of cupboard, of shelf, of glass, of her son's body. Edge of a police gun barrel, a rebel's machete, a soldier's sharp zipper. Which is to say, surviving stained her, stained her children, too.

Instead of slicing the avocado, Rafa squeezes it. He's lost in the sight of it despite the fact that he cannot feel the wet slime of it between his fingers.

You can't have him anymore, Rufina thinks. She wants to aim it at Rosalinda but swallows it instead.

The Grandmothers to All pass by the window again on their bicycles, whistling and waving, headed this time in the opposite direction, bells ringing. They rotate pedals slower uphill. An hour has lapsed since they were headed to town, and yet in this house, time feels viscous. It could've been a year. Rufina wishes her mother had been like this. A woman who rode a bicycle to the market with a clot of women strong enough to part traffic and bend laws. Who smiled instead of cried. Who knew the songs to sing to seeds so they would thrive. Who would've held her until the shards of self-doubt and confusion of girl-turning-woman worked their way out. Who would've held her. Who would've said, "My darling, how could it ever be your fault?"

It's a wish Rufina would never dare admit. Instead, she has been the one who waves from the window, from the front porch, from the drive, as the Grandmothers to All pass by.

Rosalinda, as if reading Rufina's mind, pinches her thigh.

It makes Rufina jump. "Fuck you, Ma," she says, angry that her dead mother still has the power to scare her. Angry that her dead mother still does not love her as much as she loves her brother. Angry that her mother is dead.

Rafa reaches across the table, grabbing at air as if he'll finally touch what is there, only to find it not there, again.

"Is she here?"

"Stop it," Rufina screams.

"You can see her, can't you?"

He turns on her, goes for her neck. He's slower than usual. This is his signature move, a leftover tactic from childhood.

Rufina leans back, beyond his reach. She outweighs him by flesh, heart, and will. The last time he tried to strangle her, she punched him, then held a frozen plastic bag of green chili to his face as he lay with his head in her lap, mumbling some unrecognizable combination of words. Grateful she hit him.

"Pain tells me I exist," he had said. "How many languages would you like me to translate that into?" Now Rafa is saying, "What do I have? Tell me what I have."

Seven

While the mother crouches under the table, Rafa and Rufina settle down again. They eat with their hands. Baby licks its palms. Reaches for Rufina's mouth. The walls around them appear as if they were dipped in water, painted blue, faded and streaked, darker toward the floorboards. It's as if the legs of the table, Rafa and Rufina's feet and the mother, crouching, were sliding into some unnamed body of water. It's enough to make anyone not in mourning nauseated. The gold tablecloth is faded and streaked, threadbare. The hand-stenciled design at the top of the walls, also gold and fading, is more evidence that the Explorer did exist and that he stationed himself there for a time. The kitchen was his post, where he stewed, canned, baked, sautéed, battered, and fried. The day after he left, the mother burned his apron. Rufina has gathered tulips from the yard and placed them in a collection of old mescal bottles. There are twin stems and triplet stems arcing, dark pink and purple mouths in various states of opening.

"It's like what he did to us," Rafa says, a fleck of fish hanging from his chin. "Posing us for money. His toys."

Rufina throws her napkin at him. "Wipe your face," she says. "It's not like what he did to us. We didn't want to do that. He dressed us and told us how to stand. We had to pretend there was glass between them and us. He kept all the money. And she was with us." Rufina mashes a cube of avocado in her palm with her fingernails. "We make our own decisions now. We have voices."

"It's exactly the same," Rafa says. He can see the dress rehearsal in the living room. The costumes the Explorer discovered—in thrift shops, the flea market, estate sales—and sewed to embellish. The makeup, the jewelry, the scarves and the shawls, the hats, and all the other props. He is assigning roles. There are no speaking parts.

"We're even using the same basket," Rafa says, "to collect money."

"It's not the same," Rufina says.

"We're doing it to ourselves," he says, then goes to pick at something in his teeth.

Rufina stuffs fish into her mouth. Bites at the avocado under her nails.

"But you always liked it," Rafa says, "didn't you?"

Rufina glares, then pinches her eyes shut.

The mother whimpers, which is better than the wailing. Outside, trees loiter alongside the road, blocking any starlight. Grass blankets the yard, high enough to hide the gravel kicked up from the occasional car. Skunks waddle alongside the trickle of river while raccoons wash and prepare their feasts.

When Rufina thinks Rafa isn't looking, she stomps her good leg in the direction of the mother.

"I made you," the mother says. Her voice is tar. "You exist because of me."

"That's enough," Rufina says. "No one even invited you."

"What's going on?" Rafa says. "Do you see her? Is she here?" He stands up, leans across the table.

"Look around," Rufina says. "It's just us." Her face is arranged in a way that's familiar to him. He knows better than to trust it fully.

"Tell me the truth."

"You act like she really loved you," Rufina says.

"Don't make me," he says, threatening Rufina.

Her arms lift, blocking him. "You were just her habit."

Rafa's eyes go vacant. Rufina knows he's breathing even if there isn't obvious evidence of it. Rufina knows he's gone to some memory, searching for a broken-off piece of himself. His mother is a stone, within a stone, within a stone, within a stone, at the very center of which lies his tongue.

"You're lying," he says.

The air in the room turns thick. They both know what this means. The tulips seem to point as if they were still in the ground and the sun was warming each one.

"Do you smell that?" Rufina asks her brother.

Rafa can smell the underarms of his sister's oversized T-shirt, sour-tart. He can smell the damp thicket of hair at the back of her head, above her neckline, the coconut oil.

"Copal?" he says.

They pause, ears straining. Rufina pulls Baby in tighter. Rafa sits back in his chair, crosses his legs, right thigh over left. Switches left thigh over right, and back again. He's not sure what to do with his hands, settles on folding them into a temple, and rests them on his top knee. He almost grins. He can't help himself. What can still pique his interest: the angel, and the potential of flight no matter how ragged the possibility.

"Boots," Rufina says. Rufina can hear her brother's heart beating. She can hear the saliva bubbles popping in the corners of Baby's mouth. She can hear her mother's breathing, the caustic whisper of it through nose hair.

The smell grows stronger, the sound louder. Pounding at the door. The angel does this only when she wants their full attention. Otherwise she appears and disappears unannounced. Slipping in and out as if light.

Rufina takes her cane and picks toward the sound at the front of the house. Rafa unsteeples his forefingers, smells his hands, recrosses his legs.

When Rufina returns, the angel is with her, leaning against Rufina, as if it isn't worth the trouble to stand up on her own. Dressed in stretch pants with a hole behind one of the knees, beaten steel-toe work boots, and a red T-shirt with an old Coca-Cola slogan scripted across her chest.

Rafa slides off his seat. Offers it to her.

"I'm not impressed," the angel says. She lifts the tablecloth. "Knock it off," she says to the mother, the look on her face stern.

Rafa is too distracted with the angel to sense the mother's exit. He's raking his hair back with his fingertips. Hoping this time she will let him touch the spot where the skin on her back meets the tendon of wing. Oh, how he longs to fly.

"I left the front door open for you," the angel says to the mother. It's a directive more than a suggestion. She knows the mother will slink out to the yard, linger near the well. The angel lights a Colt. The smell of burning cherries soaked in syrup diffuses into the air. Rafa is more fragile than even he knows. Notice there is what the angel will say and what the angel will not say.

Crickets crack the air with their determined notes. All the house lights are off except for a single light in the kitchen. The walls appear to be leaking. Beneath them, the mud-and-straw mixture exposed, the tulips pressing open their petals.

Under the single bulb caught in a round glass jar three feet above the table, the kitchen is the center of the universe, smelling of fish and copal, burnt eggs and moist, tired feet. It's Baby who smells like fresh-cut melon and sweet grass. Rufina adjusts the rebozo Baby is tucked inside. Angel's and Baby's eyes meet. Baby squirms and wiggles, arches its back.

Rufina sees the angel's gaze fall on Baby. "Please don't," Rufina says.

The angel has warned Rufina about Baby. Everything, she has said, has an expiration date.

When the angel decides to make Baby disappear, it takes days for Rufina to find it again. She's had to clean out every corner of the house, dig in the yard, tear into the trunks of trees, tie a rope around her waist and make Rafa lower her into the well. Each time, it's more difficult. Rufina blames the angel for everything. After all, she first appeared on that morning when Rufina gave birth to Baby.

The angel turns the chair backward, straddles it cowboy-style, places her hands on her crotch, adjusts herself.

"Fifteen dollars?" Rufina says. She points to the wallet on the table.

The angel nods her head.

"Fifty in the basket?" Rufina says.

Rafa scratches at the tattoo over his heart. "You want me to win, don't you?"

"I stood all day," Rufina says. "Do you hear how hoarse my voice is? And I worked the crowd. I engaged them. I didn't just stand there."

"I saw that," the angel says.

"You could turn up the speaker," Rafa says, his voice a calm attack. "Better yet, use a microphone that works. You have a cane. Lean on it. Undo a button or two. You know how to pose, how to lure. Pot of gold. *My Little Pot of Gold.* Isn't that what he used to call you? In German, in Italian, in Turkish. It didn't matter what language. You would prance and squeal like he was crowning you queen." He glances at the angel, trying to decipher her expression.

The veins on Rufina's neck are pulsing wires. She wraps her hair around her wrist, ties it into a knot on top of her head. "No one wants you to win our bet, except you." She's ready to spit. Her aim is just as good as the mother's. Still, arguing is familiar. A sign of devotion. She prepares herself for the battle. They are fierce. They are alive.

"I went, didn't I? I stole the wallet." He pushes himself onto the counter. Sits on his hands. "That's something."

The angel adjusts her headband. Her wings arc up over her head and quake. It's nothing more than a stretch. The wings are a fragile, sinewy mess, a puzzle of functionality. Rafa tracks their every move.

"It doesn't matter," Rafa says. He's done. That quick. Nothing for Rufina to tear into after all.

"It might matter," says the angel. "Might not."

"Is that all you have to say?" Rufina says. She's never been particularly fond of the angel's communication skills or lack thereof.

Rafa could almost reach out and pet the one rebel feather poking out the top of her wing.

"How about being useful?" Rufina says, clapping her hands. "Instead of posing." She continues to clap as if directing a yard full of chickens.

"That's enough for now," the angel says, standing.

"You think?" Rufina says, trailing close behind the angel as she makes for the front door, which she quickly exits and slams in Rufina's face. "You don't have anything else to say?" Rufina screams into the wood and paint. "How about helping us out instead of watching us suffer?"

The angel crosses through the yard, hiccupping. Rafa paces the table. Around and around. The mother, outside at the well, paces in the opposite direction, around and around.

In the mother's homeland, there was a volcano, and at the top there was a lake, and at the bottom of the lake there was a hole, and through the hole was a tunnel that led to all those who had come before. Know this: There were stories recorded in the mother's body. They were present at her birth and present at her death even if she didn't know how to tell them.

Rufina doesn't realize what she's invoking. Prayers, demands, requests have a hundred thousand ways of being answered.

Rufina clicks her cane down the hall into the darkness, into her bedroom, shuts her door, commits the lock. The window is open and at ground level. Still, something about locking the door. From the top of her dresser, she takes two shells, "Just like the ones from the shore of the lake where your people come from," he had told her. She had placed them next to the dried marigolds, the gourds, the crystals, the glass jars of buttons and beads, and, stuffed in a tin bucket, her collection of antique hand mirrors, the glass stained and warped in each one. *Can you see yourself?* he had asked her. *Look how beautiful you are.* She steps over her clothes, strung across the floor like a rope bridge. She leans against the headboard, Baby at her chest. After she places the shells in Baby's palms, Baby shakes its fists. There is no sound.

"Monday morning he's gone," she whispers. "It must be so. And you and I will stay and wait." Rufina traces the rim of Baby's nose and chin. "I am here for you and you are here for me. Together we are a family."

Baby taps the shells against its mouth. Hisses. Its eyes are bright a moment, but then the lids grow heavy.

Baby sleeps curled on Rufina's stomach. Rafa is at Rufina's door longing to smell a woman who is related to him, longing to smell her on his skin. He wants to feel that close to himself, which he cannot feel when he's alone.

In the night, Baby wants milk, but instead sucks on the ends of Rufina's hair. Breast milk is an old story told to others, but not to Baby. Baby pushes off, slinks down the length of the bed. Gums its hand. Slinks back again, curls onto Rufina's chest. Watches her breathe.

Down the hall, in the kitchen, the mother pulls each plate from the cupboard. All the different sizes, all the different colors. She marks the house with them. Makes a path on the floor. One ceramic moon after another to step on. This is how to know you're going in the right direction. This is how they can find you, should you manage to escape. She was told, stay out of sight. She was told, mark your path. Here is the path. This is how they will find her. This is how she will remember where she's been. These are her tracks. She was here.

Eight

It was the third Saturday of June, the first day of summer. Rafa was nine, Rufina seven. They paraded with the mother into the small city, like they did most Saturdays. Rufina, the tallest with the longest gait. Notice how both hips were stable, equal, both were once beautiful and strong. Rafa held the mother's sewing to the center of his chest. Rufina cradled the mother's ink drawings—mounted on squares of wood and individually wrapped in cloth napkins—stacked in a box that was cumbersome to carry, not because of its weight, as it was fairly light, but because it was twice as long as it was wide. She managed by setting it down to switch her grip every few yards. While she did this, she waited for the other two.

Then, she would start off again. The mother, holding her elbows, was the last to rejoin.

As they crossed the plaza, the mother's skirt billowed—a kite too close to the earth. A grass woven hat shielded her eyes; the cloak of her hair fell past her waist in a thick, black expanse. Modern women scurried around her with their curled, lacquered hair, nails filed and polished into points, tight denim cutting into hip creases while they balanced on the tips of their high heels. Simple gold crosses strung around their necks. They avoided the mother. Refused to make eye contact. She noted their shadows moving across the ground.

Rosalinda had lived here for nearly ten years, and still, every time she entered the plaza, she would stop and take it all in as if it were the day she'd arrived. She did so on this day as well. The cottonwood trees were so massive and commanding, it was as if they were pinning the plaza to the earth. Crows flicked and twirled through the air on their jaunts above. Day laborers passed through, hurrying to clock in. The Original Enduring Ones tended to their wares and watched, amused. Tourists coerced by turquoise, painted boots, and cowboy hats hauled bags, bought more and more, argued about price. The adobe storefront walls facing the plaza created edges, not unlike a box. Inside the plaza, families sprawled out on the grass, lapping at ice cream cones. In the center, a fountain with multiple tiers of concrete bowls brimming with water, coins lining the bottom. The mother slipped off her shoes, stepped onto a bench, toes gripping wooden slats, palms balancing on each child's head, and surrendered her eyes to the sight of the mountains both near and far. She inhaled deeply, pulling all that she could see down deep inside her body. The strength of the mountains. The strength of the sky. It was not where she was from, this was true, but it was her home. She had claimed it and we could say it claimed her as well.

She was alive.

Her children were alive.

She had a son, in whose face she saw her father's and her grandfathers' faces, her brothers' and uncles' faces. Men who had done their best to protect her. There were the gifts of the house, the garden, the rain every afternoon during monsoons that blessed her whether she believed she deserved it or not. Her memory had grown over with scar tissue, which meant the function of her mind kept to the pathways that were most useful, most relevant. And her body, the small, sturdy package of it, was a paradox of fierce survival and fragility. But in this place, Ciudad de Tres Hermanas, she could pretend she understood what it meant to be safe.

The gallery owners wanted to know why the mother's portraits were so mournful. Again, the same images?

Who were these people supposed to be, anyway? What else did she have to show? Any animals? Landscapes sold well.

These questions did not keep Rosalinda from making the weekly visits with her portraits to the various galleries occupying nearly every street in the city. It did not keep the gallery owners from asking the same questions. It did not keep them from saying no. She would point to the portraits of her family, all of them men. All of them gone. The value of a family taken, wasted. "Look at their faces," she'd tell them. "Don't you see animals? Don't you see landscapes?"

They wanted to know if she was Indian. They could promote her along with the others if that was the case. They'd have a better idea of what to do with her, although if she could do one with a coyote or a buffalo, that would help.

"Not your kind of Indian," she had told them. "Not the kind in the movies."

Her face was marked by her people, people who lived high in the mountains with the steady music of rain, the unimaginable palette of birds, and where orchids seemed to form in midair, where trees created vast tents over the land. This was where the volcano rose up. In its crater, the lake; at the bottom, through the hole, down the tunnel, was the dwelling place. In the dwelling place lived the uninterrupted memory of the people. There's no way for you to know that this dwelling place was where the stories they sang and repeated to one another and to themselves lived. It's likely you understand this as metaphor. Because of this tendency to rely on your mental constraints, you will never truly understand. Inside your bones are the cells that can feel the vibration of all kinds of stories. Their humming often escapes you. This is not entirely your fault, but the disbelief is. Start there.

Rosalinda's ink drawings were not purchased. They were never purchased. Still, she insisted on painting them. In addition, she sewed intricate hand stitches that shamed any machine. The shop that commissioned her sewing was unnamed. Hardly larger than a closet, it was full of racks of alterations in various stages of completion. Above the racks, folded stacks of material rose to the ceiling. Beneath the racks, bins of scrap material, thread, buttons, and the like. The shop was impeccably ordered but the lack of natural light and the corroded wood floor made it unwelcoming. A pale woman, smaller than the mother, ran the shop, Doña Allegre. She barely spoke to the mother or Rafa, or Rufina. Her eyes seemed habitually focused on a faraway point, while the orders stacked on the counter dwarfed her even further. Despite the shop's looks, and its lack of a name, everyone knew its mending was unparalleled.

On this first day of summer, while Rafa sat on the floor picking at a scab on his knee, and Rufina rifled through a bin, searching for a new button to slip into her pocket, the mother stood next to a man with a costume in his arms, holding it as if he were holding a sick child. He towered above her, an alabaster pillar, his smile overwhelming. She'd never seen a man smile like that, with all of himself, his eyes in on it, too. His whole body, it seemed, was in on it. He had asked her if she could fix the tears in the dress. He explained it was for a series of installation pieces in which he'd been staging mannequins in the most surprising places around town—in parks, in arroyos, on the corners of busy intersections, even in parked cars left on the side of the road. He outfitted them in layers of mixed, and often contrary, inspiration. Collaging them, he'd said. As if remote parts of the world, with its remote citizens, had landed on one figure. One of his favorite pieces was a male mannequin in a gas mask, an Inuit coat, several Hawaiian leis. And on the bottom half, a Scottish kilt with flippers meant for snorkeling.

"It's art, you see," he'd said, rocking the dress in his arms. "It's about making an impact." Then, again, his smile shining. All his shining teeth. His skin and head shining under the caustic fluorescent lights of the shop.

The mother had avoided men. The last time she'd permitted a man to kiss her, she'd become pregnant with Rufina.

No men needed. She had a son. She had Rafa. That was enough.

"Please. If you'd be so kind," the man pleaded, extending the torn dress. "I'd pay double, of course."

She looked at Rafa, whose scab was bleeding, and at Rufina, who was filling her pockets with buttons. She looked again at the man, at his hands twisted and swollen with arthritis. Slowly, she nodded. And when he found out she'd come on foot, he packed her things into the trunk of his Chevy Citation, ushered the children into the backseat, opened the passenger door for her, and set out for the canyon.

"My goodness," he'd said as he drove the last mile to the house. The yellow rose bushes alongside the road were thick with blossoms, melted over with bees. The air from the open windows tugged at their skin. "What good fortune."

Nine

◆

Rafa is desperate to be close to his sister. All his senses are detecting the mother, and yet, there is nothing he can hold. The walls of the house feel pressurized. Panic is caught in his chest—it flutters. After trying her locked door, Rafa climbs in through Rufina's open window. He walks across her room, his feet pacing as if on some distant shore. Baby pins him with its eyes, pulls on Rufina's hair, which makes her breathing change, makes her shift, swim her legs. Rafa lies on the floor. His head pillowed on Rufina's discarded skirt and bundle of blouse. He can smell every moment of the day in her clothes. The moment she strained her throat to hit a note she hadn't known existed, the moment she threw her left hip forward for too long, her right shoulder leaning back to make a bow of her body, arching. He can smell when she held her bladder for too long, where she was in her cycle. He smells the sweetness and the foulness of her, rubs his face in it. Dizzies himself. Feels somehow closer to the mother because of this. Falls asleep. Baby is nestled on Rufina's chest, its neck a hinge, its face opening toward Rafa. Eyes ever present, tiny mirrors. Blinding.

When the mother finishes with the plates, she gathers the glasses and the bowls, turns each one upside down. Arranges them in rows of four as close to the walls as she can get, makes triangles on the rug in the front room with the utensils, and on the rug down the hall, rectangles and X's.

The angel leans against the elm across the road at the bottom of the hill—the land pulses. She scares a swarm of dragonflies from their restless sleep, stares up at the house. The canyon is aware of the house and what happens inside. They understand each other's place. It has always been and will always be this way. The air is spiked with alertness.

If you slow and quiet yourself, you'll notice water bubbling up from the ground. You'll feel, beneath your feet, hidden in the soil, the movement of seeds constellated like stars, the webbing of roots. Try orienting yourself this way. The future happens in multiple directions and what came before is always embedded. It's quite possible you will not understand how the canyon is a living, breathing presence. How the house is a living, breathing presence. A presence that sees and knows, feels, hears. It holds them all—Baby, the brother, the sister, the mother, and memories of the Explorer. The house holds lifetimes, real and imagined, living and deceased.

The angel climbs through Rufina's open window, first one exceptionally long leg, then the other. As she shakes out her wings, a spray of mites litters the floor. She sees what is not here: Rufina, age ten, at her desk, cutting out images of landscapes from photography books, gluing them together. She sees what is not here: Rufina, age twelve, brushing her hair before wrapping it in a long scarf, knotting it at the back of her head, singing. Lucio Armijo clipping up the drive to his post outside her window. Two chile rellenos fat as hearts, wrapped in a paper towel, the grease already soaked through, the batter already cold and soft. His need to provide and protect stronger than it ever should be at that age. Rufina, age fourteen, in bed, seven months pregnant, commissioned to embroider the collar of a woman's blouse. Doña Allegre surprisingly supportive with the sewing tasks she gave to Rufina. "You're fatter than my girls ever got with their firsts," she'd said when she'd dropped the work off at the house. Tiny Christmas lights strung in a mess from the ceiling, as if a clump of galaxy. A tapestry like the one her mother's people could have made is draped on the wall behind her bed. A series of black ink portraits her mother painted, that no one ever wanted, fills one entire wall. Family Rufina would never meet. Not like Rafa's or Rufina's fathers. Men worth knowing.

The mother on her hands and knees in the front room continues arranging butter knives along the thresholds, zigzags them, hums. Saucers come next, then wooden spoons. In the morning, like every morning, the sink and dish rack will be empty, as will the drawers on either side of the stove, the bottom cupboards as well as the top cupboards. Rufina is always first to find and return them to their proper places. Erasing her mother's tracks. While Rosalinda finishes, she speaks to herself in a language her children had once accused her of making up. What do they know about her language? Not like those languages Rafa learned, that all sounded the same, like the Explorer's languages. There were stories she was told. There was a particular way in which they were told. They were to be used as medicine. She was to carry them with her. They would keep her alive. They would keep her children alive. This is what her mother had told her when she journeyed with her to the top of the volcano, at the shore of the lake, when she blessed Rosalinda. Years later, when she escaped, the stories were the first thing to be stripped from her along with her people's name and her name. Never to return. All her life and never once did the stories return. No matter how hard she tried to force them, no matter all the different ways she tried making them up.

Now, to remember her steps in the dark there is a saucer, a glass, a bowl. A way to keep track. How many of these will equal the distance to her birthplace? Which configuration will unlock her ability to trace what has gone missing in her memory? If she uses enough plates and utensils, where will it take her? Back in time? To her village? That far? Or will it take her to him, to the Explorer, again? Such an ordinary thing, a kitchen and what's used there to support the task of eating, to support the daily effort of living—and yet, not one item does Rosalinda take for granted. Her hand on each item is a comfort, and there is so little of that. Her body is brittle. Nothing will cradle her with as much tenderness as she needs. Not even her son can hold her. Her joints are marbles trying to roll away from her. Why does everything want to escape her?

✦

In addition to seeing what is not there now, the angel also sees what is there. Rufina nursing her own shadow with a dry breast. Unconsciously, in her sleep. Rafa flopped on his sister's clothes. Breaking open, breaking apart. Remember this, everyone needs to be careful.

The angel sits on the trunk at the end of the bed, hiccupping. Signals to Baby. If only the coyotes lapping at the trickle of river would cry, like they have done so many times before, offer a warning for Rufina and wake her, but instead, it is a vast kind of quiet. Know this: The only thing the angel loves more than Baby is Rufina. In no time, Baby is in the angel's lap, like a charm. It weighs more than the angel. It trills, curls it toes.

Ten

◈

The angel is out the window, down the drive, past the water, into the hills, beyond the tree line, wings begging purchase, as if the whole contraption of her functions by some unseen hand crank. There now, she rises and is carried along. The Grandmothers to All witness this commotion in the night sky as they light candles and climb into the trees.

The angel will be back before morning to catch the mother and force her down the well in the backyard. You know, of course, why this has to happen now. The angel has bent toward the broken pleas of Rafa and Rufina for years, enabled them for far too long. Both of them now are capable of being eaten by their insistent grief.

It threatens to swallow both of them whole. The angel knows this just like you know it.

Meanwhile, down below, under more heavens than can be counted, Rufina dreams of the Grandmothers to All, which in her dream look not like their wrinkled, pale versions, but instead resemble her unknowable ancestors. Rather than riding bicycles, they are perched on rocks. They scrub Rufina with red willow bundles. Their hands pull her hair, her fingertips, her ears, her breasts. They pound her knees, her feet. She is mud. She is being made. The volcano is sacred earth, towering above. They are howling. "Oh baby, return."

It's quite possible you will not understand how Rufina could trust the bet she made less than Rafa, who doesn't trust it at all. Pay attention to how she resists this knowing. She does not want Rafa dead; she does want him out of the canyon, out of town. She wants to dig into the house for the rest of her days and nurse—one breast for her dead baby, one for her dead mother, who for Rufina are always present. Which is to say, she wants to dig into the reality her memory provides. Let's not forget this is where the Explorer still exists and the couple she wanted so badly to call mother and father. While she doesn't know the volcano, or the lake, or what dwells in the bottom, let alone comprehend the language her mother and her ancestors spoke, she still has the instincts. From her bloodstream, her ancestors still call to her. There is what needs to be remembered and embraced. She has no idea when she sings, "Return," that it's her own strength she's calling to.

Rafa must go. This is true. He's almost done it before. Pills. Handfuls of them. Swallowed, then brought back up. This small city, this canyon, this house has had that effect on him. Time and time again. It's only when he's traveling on a plane or is on an island that he's calm. When he can draw the edges of land, quite easily located, on a napkin at the shoreside bar of such a place, then the great surrender. Full breaths. The water helps, he's not sure how.

Notice how desperate he is to be held. At night, when he curls on the floor of Rufina's room, he's waiting for her to wake and invite him into her twin bed, her childhood bed. It's Baby who takes up too much space. A force he cannot see but feels strongly. Its force keeping him from getting too close. And yet, he feels more crippled than his sister with her limp and her cane when there's no one to embrace him.

The containment of arms. The containment of land.

What he sees is the angel, who appeared at Baby's birth and has always lingered.

Never mind Rufina hasn't thought this weekend through. Never mind the angel knows exactly what she's planning and will never let it happen.

Here's the difficulty with rescue: It's more demanding for you than anyone else. Which is to say, while everyone has a role, if you don't take the lead in your own saving, everything and everyone will be damned, including you.

Rosalinda knew very little as she traversed territories and borders as she headed north, but she knew this: If she gave up, no amount of assistance would matter. Remember this.

Officer Armijo has been put in charge of enforcing permits this weekend. Difficult with these two, given his record of loving Rufina. He loved her when he was a boy. Waiting outside her bedroom window, just like he waited for her at school. He loved her when he was getting married and when he had his first son. And he loves her still, but not in the way you think. Not in the way of sinking into her, planting himself, and claiming her. Not in any way she could possibly imagine. A love that doesn't need or want anything in return. There is desire, it's true, but know this, Lucio Armijo always has been and always will be in awe of Rufina Rivera.

Rafa can't get himself to imagine living without his mother's arms. He'll never understand the way in which a small island and all that water re-creates the feeling he had in baths he took with her. Until that last one, of course. He can barely finish a sentence worth any importance, but don't let this fool you. He has something deep in there itching to live that he doesn't know about. It could go either way.

The angel is all about pushing at this point. Similar to when she sat on the trunk at the end of Rufina's bed when Rufina was fourteen and Baby was crowning.

The angel had willed Rufina to push as Rafa cried, holding his sister's head, his tears dripping on her face. The Grandmothers to All crowded Rufina's room with plant potions and prayers while the mother sat in the rocking chair on the roof. The angel is about pushing. Rufina will be pushed and Rafa will be pushed and one of them, or both of them, or neither of them will sprout the skill they need for the next part of their lives, which by the way has grown weary with waiting.

Notice the house. Like a loyal family pet, ever patient, unconditional. Notice how it softens edges of walls, loosens locks, dims the corners, allows Rosalinda to make a mess with the dishes without disturbing anyone. Stays so very quiet. Only the house measures each gesture of longing as equal. Gathers these gestures, records them. It's the house that continues to provide shelter to all despite living or dead, continues holding, regardless. And the shadows writhing in Rufina's bedroom—all those ink portraits on the wall and what they have seen, even the mirror forced to reflect the misfortune—still, the house tries to protect her as best a house can.

The house knows many things, knows east and west, north and south. Knows how to listen. Hears the laughter, the wailing and the pleading. The house knows how to cradle whomever is inside, knows how to nurse simultaneous stories. It seems as if the house birthed itself and rebirthed itself over centuries, one layer of mud plaster after another. It is older than any municipal archive. It knew they would be coming even before they could imagine such a thing—the brother, the sister, the mother, the Explorer.

Saturday

One

◇

When Rufina wakes, she focuses her sight on the sunlit wall, where a crude pattern of lace curtain is projected. She's sweating. Fists behind her neck, legs knotted at the knees. Her head aches with confusion. Her mother is deceased, but refuses to leave; her rescue plan for Rafa may or may not be interrupted by Officer Armijo; after one day of performing for the tourists, they have a wallet with countless receipts and fifteen dollars cash; the angel that stalks her refuses to manifest any spectacular acts, refuses to answer any of her prayers. Rufina presses this list of worries to the back of her throat. Her hip throbs. It feels twice its size, dense and heavy, as if packed with wet sand. The temptation to let the pain pin her to her bed for the day is overwhelming.

Baby is not in the crook of her lower back, nor on the pillow next to her, its head on her cheek, breath puffing against her neck. Her brother is no longer on the floor, fileted like some sacrificial lamb—curls greasy, shadows printed under his eyes, drool on his chin, limbs flopped this way and that. Once the mother had settled, the house opened, his panic dissipated, Rafa had climbed back out through the window, his bare feet on the dirt. He'd settled on the couch under the apricot tree as dawn neared.

Heaviness settles in her lungs. Dread is a slow act of suffocation. Her mind races to a pleasant moment. It's an act of self-preservation. She remembers herself twelve and waking on a Saturday morning. She goes into the kitchen. There's the Explorer, apron-clad, making breakfast. Whipped cream, sliced and spiced fruit, links of browned chorizo, pancakes, thin and crisp, all piled high and ready for the pillaging. There are the kisses he was so generous with, one at each of her temples, this was her blessing when she appeared at his side. She can feel the weight of his arm around her shoulders, the bristles of hair on his forearm against the skin of her neck. She can see, in one corner of the kitchen, the mother's sewing machine. A mound of material is heaped on a nearby bench, a separate pile for the hand-stitched work. Draped on a velvet hanger, suspended from a nail in one of the vigas above, is the dress he picked for Rufina to wear for the day's performance. And in the opposite corner to the sewing machine, Rosalinda. Cigarette at a sharp diagonal secured in the corner of her mouth as she balances on a stool. Scraps of cloth pieced and pinned together on her body, necessary for creating the perfect fit. The Explorer and his perfect fits. There is Rafa hovering at her feet, having completed the task of polishing her toenails a shade of distressed copper, not unlike the color of her skin. There is Rafa tying the silk ribbons into her braids and wrapping the ends in bells. Her headdress of giant paper flowers, waiting. And listen, there is the soundtrack. One of the Explorer's records twirling sound. Voices never singing in English.

Rufina continues to remember this childhood routine—when they acted like a family, they were a family—as she forces herself to sit on the edge of her bed. See how easy it is for her to be a girl again with a family? She can put herself there once more, make it so.

Her mind fights her, and it's thoughts of Baby that force her to lift the sheet and the pillow, scanning for a sign. She lowers herself to her hands and knees and peers beneath the bed. No Baby. She reaches for her cane, and with it in hand, her movements quicken. Her robe sways open as she makes her way down the hall. Sweat dampens her skin. She has a whistle she uses for Baby, teeth against bottom lip, tongue curled, more inhale than exhale, a breathy soft sound. The floor of the house, littered with dishes, makes it difficult to step cleanly. She picks her way through, her cane knocking over a glass and splitting it. She uses her cane to sweep the assortments out of her way. Her racket upsets the quiet of the house. It sounds as if everything is breaking. She gathers the dishes, throwing them into the sink. Morning sun rings the floor. As she steps toward its spotlight with one foot, she drags the other leg behind her. Baby is not in the hall on one of the shelves, not on the couch or under the couch, not on the table, not in any of the cupboards.

It is not only Baby who cannot to be found, but Rosalinda, also seems to be missing. She's not hanging around on the hallway floor or out circumambulating the well, or in the rocking chair on the roof.

Instead of Baby or Rosalinda, Rufina has found Rafa in the yard. Rufina spies his feet, dirtier than the soles of worn shoes, jutting out past the cushions of the couch. The pointed rays of the morning sun nearly reaching him.

Baby's absence is a physical pain that increases in intensity. This makes it harder for Rufina to breathe. She tries to soothe herself, but instead, her breathing speeds, becomes sharp, stops, and then restarts with gasping. She knows that no matter where she searches—in the back of all the closets and all the cupboards, under the sink, behind the toilet, on the roof, in both woodpiles—Baby will still be missing. The house cannot give her what she is desperate for. Instead, it prepares itself for what will be.

One.

Two.

Three.

This is how she reasons with her panic.

One. Never mind the mother for now. She is an impossible feat of immortality.

Two. She will drag Rafa off the couch and through the yard, if need be. She will douse him with peppermint water, hand him a salted corn tortilla with butter, and a jar of coffee with milk and honey, shove his hat down on his head, push him all the way down the hill to the plaza if she has to. But not before she sorts through everything he's touched. Not before she's discovered a fresh stash of pills. She will not let him die, too. She *will not*.

Three. When the angel appears, as she always does, there will be an answer for Baby. Rufina will not surrender to the feeling that burns within the center of her as if she had choked down a live coal, which instead of cooling, only intensifies in heat. Instead, she will dress herself, tug the little red wagon, claim their section of the plaza, unleash her noises, perform, collect money.

And he will live.

Two

By 11 a.m. a densely packed circle has formed around the brother-sister duo. The tourists are disoriented by the time change. Is it still breakfast? How long until dinner? Have we missed our guided tour? Is it too early to drink tequila? The heels of their shoes strangle the life out of the grass. It's shredded, bent into dirt. They shift and kick, unaware as trail horses. They stare as if the world exists for their viewing alone, objects arranged for their pleasure. The crows have returned as well. Hopping from one tree limb to another, gossiping about the ravens' takeover of all the flat-topped roofs. Never mind how endless the sky, and the moon—almost complete—now ghosted by the sun.

Twenty foreheads shine in the late morning light.

Shifty hips. Small, pale children. Fingers, reaching for mother, father. To Rufina, the ring of tourists does not consist of people, breathing beings; rather they appear to her as a painted set design. Poorly constructed at that, all of it one-dimensional, especially what she sees in their eyes when they look at her. We could say she is guilty of seeing herself this way as well. She fixes her gaze beyond them, on the mountains anchored in every direction— thirty miles, seventy miles, one hundred miles away— feels how deliberate their evolution, how stubborn they are in their magnitude. Somehow this reminds her of Baby, and the burning panic inside her ignites again, shifts her breathing to panting.

Rafa concentrates on the guitar, specifically, on the place where the strings should be. Wonders how to summon sound. Only an hour ago, he'd stumbled behind his sister as she screamed at him, "You promised. You fucking promised." He holds the guitar up high, as if it were a rifle he were aiming at the stars. There, for him to contemplate, is the hole in the middle, a portal into emptiness. He considers the notion of belonging.

At one moment, following Rufina into town, through the patch of woods next to the river, he'd glimpsed the back of the mother. Her rope of braid. Her small hips. It was as if she were real again, not a mirage confined by the walls of the house, but still existing in the world at large and everything around him flushed into its full animating force. There were his feet on the ground. The weight of his steps. He could hear a variety of sounds. Birdsong, water moving, leaves shushing. Then it was gone as fast as it came.

Now, as he grips the guitar, he stares into the hole. Inside him, his own portal, he can feel it, an exposed opening that nothing can properly fill, aching and inept, like a mouth that has recently lost all of its teeth. He wears the same thing he wore the day before, smelling of rancid creases, the crowded, unkempt kitchen, Rufina's floor, the mother's bedroom, and the peppermint oil that Rufina insisted on as she pulled him out the door and down the lane. He grips his hat, lowering it. The feathers littering the rim fan out in all directions. He scans the ground on which the tourists are standing. Images shimmer in the shadows. He squints. Tries to bring something in all the darkness into focus, wonders about the possible translations. Feels himself dissolving in the concentration of this act.

Above, the crows continue to call, settling into tree limbs. A tide of day laborers passes by in pickups—the front seats thick with bodies—on the way from one side of town to the other, the living side to the working side. "Did you see the way . . ." their stories begin. "If I had that compound . . ." their stories continue, ending with "Even the dog was giving orders! Chingada!" And there are those on foot scrambling from one restaurant to

BROTHER, SISTER, MOTHER, EXPLORER

another, fingers pruned, hands chapped, endless buckets of water, which surround them even in their dreams. They slip into back doors as customers marvel at centerpieces made of fry bread. Foreign shop clerks stand amid clouds of cologne in front of their adobe storefronts selling genuine handmade jewelry from China. Meanwhile, the Original Enduring Ones shift on their lawn chairs, rearrange the goods on their blankets, explain a design for the hundred thousandth time, speak of the symbols. This one means thunder. This one means rain. This one means spider. A joke starts at one end of the line of vendors, tumbles down nearly forty yards to the other end. You can listen for the wave of laughter as it moves and chart the joke's success. Note the intensity. The flute deity decorates every possible wearable item. Notice he is missing his bundle and his erection. He is no longer holy. The tourists are unaware of this castration of his power. The tourists are unaware of power lost. How will they ever care enough to learn? And who will teach them?

Three

◇

Around the periphery of the plaza, the angel lurks with those legs of hers. Her wings are snug, one on top of the other, and resting against her back. They continue past her hips, tapering off at her upper thighs, not unlike a feathered cape. Here and there, a row of spines quiver as if shot through with electricity. Tips curling and uncurling. She pauses behind the man who twists balloons into animals, a mouse, a giraffe, a bear. Watches the faces of the children as they try to guess what creature will appear, which one will be theirs to take home. All of their small hands extended, expectant. Palms facing up.

"I like it," one child says about a balloon that could be a snail.

"Me, too," says another.

"You can give it to me," says a third. "It's my favorite."

The parents, both mothers and fathers, attempt to rein in their children, discourage them from overtly begging. They flash awkward smiles meant to apologize while the man twisting the balloon skins tight with air says, "Not to worry." A nose appears, ears, a tail. The friction of his manipulations cause a series of squeaks that excites the children even more. "Not to worry," he repeats.

It's quite the trick. Turning one thing into another. The angel scans the plaza. There is Rafa and Rufina, straining against the expectations of the crowd, straining against the uncertainty of the bet.

On the angel's wrist, digital numbers read:

10:37 am
Sat. 5.30

Four

◈

The husband and the wife are back. They are the kind of people who mean what they say, for better or for worse. The husband in his long shorts. The wife in her new matching turquoise necklace and earrings, her other beige summer blouse. No matter how hard he searched, the husband never did find his wallet. What he cannot imagine: It is still propped open like a miniature book on the kitchen floor of the house, untouched overnight even by the mother. Before the couple left their room and made their way to the plaza, the wife had listed all the significant things the husband had lost since they'd been married. Gone were their matching monogram slippers, and the garage door opener, his, hers, and the spare. Gone was the fancy wine bottle opener his brother gifted

them for their twenty-fifth wedding anniversary. The
husband had continued to search for his wallet as the
wife lectured him. It had been better than sitting still.
He preferred to be a moving target. The wife blamed the
husband. When it was his turn, the husband blamed the
wife.

They have not spoken yet today. He follows her and
her purse around, careful not to strike out on his own.
Cursing her in his mind but afraid to leave her side. Today is not nearly as enchanting as the day before in Ciudad de Tres Hermanas.

Upon spotting Rufina, the wife says, "Look. There."
To the wife, Rufina is the kind of woman who is not
the least bit concerned with how others perceive her. A
woman who clearly hasn't tamed her own hair into some
kind of style, let alone brushed it, who is in need of shav-
ing her armpits and her legs, whose clothes don't match.
It both frustrates and excites her.

The husband sees Rufina and blushes. To him, Rufina
is the kind of woman who would never exist in his reality. A woman who would no doubt bite him, given the
chance, who doesn't cross her legs when she sits, who he
imagines could make him hard or limp on command. It
both frustrates and excites him.

"Are you turning red?" the wife asks him. She can
see the way her husband is tracking Rufina, a kind of
stalking men do with their eyes and think is unnoticeable,

harmless. "Still embarrassed from the stunt you pulled yesterday?"

"Your breath," he says. "Smells like mustard." He clearly is avoiding the wife's question. "It stinks," he continues. "Why do you have to eat everything?"

She has a tin full of mints in her purse, but does not reach for them. She says, "It's not mustard. It's Southwest spice-flavored piñon nuts. You could at least try being adventurous while we're here. It's only temporary."

"Please don't breathe with your mouth open," he says. "It's intolerable."

At a forlorn hour the previous night they had lain awake, back to back, beneath the blanket arguing about how much to pay the duo, thinking they were married, not siblings. The husband insisted on no more than fifty dollars. The wife wouldn't hear of anything less than eighty, two twenties for them each.

"Did you see how badly he needed to bathe?" the wife had argued. "Did you not notice how scrappy her dress was? It's the least we can do."

When the husband would not agree to her donation price, she switched to another battery of insults, a list of all the things the husband should've felt guilty about since they'd been married. The last words he heard as he held the pillow over his head were "You ought to be ashamed."

Now, he huffs and puffs as if preparing to shout at her, then shrinks. The air inside him escapes, makes a sound not unlike the smallest squeak of a balloon being stretched into shape. "It's not my fault you don't like me anymore," he says.

Not replying is a kind of forgiveness she gives him every time he behaves this way.

"She looks like she's going to collapse," the wife says, routing the attention to Rufina.

Rufina has yet to sing. The broken microphone is ornamentation, a convincing prop. She'll have to force the amplification of her voice without assistance. The red dress she's wearing scallops her neck, hugs her lumps, grabs her thighs, and falls two inches past her knees. A pattern of pink and yellow rose embroidery, the size of Baby's palms, presses down her chest and around her waist. She wears sunglasses, two ovals cut from dark purple plastic. Her lips are naked and splitting from the dry heat. Her hair—countless curls—frizzes loose down her back. Her right foot stomps a rectangle cookie sheet. When the block of her wooden heel strikes, another universe explodes. Strung around her left ankle, bells. In her left hand, castanets; in her right hand, finger cymbals. There is a kind of rhythm, but only if you listen closely.

Her earrings drop past her shoulders, thin strips cut from hide. They curl away from her collarbones at the tips. Tourists mistake her for a fairy tale. The wandering maiden cursed to roam forever, lost in the woods. She has no magic wand, no godmother willing to turn her life into the best version possible, and no prince trapped in the body of a toad, or an old white man, or any other creature.

"That clanging is hideous," the husband says.

The couple does not move. In their matching short pants, they stand as if waiting for their punishment. The husband wants Rufina's dress to split. He wants her exposed so he can truly measure her, uninterrupted, against what he pictures in his mind.

On Rufina's tongue, "Oh, my baby, return," but she will not part her lips. Her eyes, each one, a puddle filling. Her jaw has locked. She tries to imagine where Baby has gone. Her body won't hold the rhythm steady. It fights against her will. The crowd seems to collectively tilt its head, curious whether she can maintain her calculations, but the way their mouths are pursed, and the palpable shrinking of attention, suggest it's unlikely. The basket is empty except for the crystal Rufina put there and some coins.

Rafa continues to watch shadows. He sees different combinations in the images. The sage, the outlaw, the child, the royal figures, the magician, or the lover, all of whom might be accompanied by a goat, a skunk, a snake, a hummingbird, or a spider, placed in or near a tree, a field, a pond, an orchard, a hut. There was usually weather and possibly other signifiers he might or might not detect given how clearly he could see on any particular day. As the husband and wife approach, he sees in her shadow that the goat from the day before dangles from the lowest limb by its hind legs, the drizzling rain has transformed into a deluge, and the crown hangs from a branch just out of her reach. In the husband's shadow is the outlaw, knife drawn, bare feet, bare hands in a fog-veiled field overrun with skunks under a waxing moon. Rafa cannot remember what skunks en masse means.

Speakers pulse from open windows. Cars roll at 15 m.p.h. around the plaza. Chicano Kings. Norteño Kings. See how low they can go. An all-girls mariachi band spills out of a convertible, yipping and wailing—hair slick, crimson-rimmed mouths, hands furious on instruments. The sign advertising their next show is marked on poster board and fixed to the driver's and passenger's doors. The man driving the car wears black sunglasses and a gray felt fedora. The woman next to him lifts her chin and chest, stares out above the heads of those standing on the street, as if she, too, were about to break into a storm of gritos. The tiniest of papel flores booths is overturned by the direct hit of a poorly aligned stroller. A father on his cell phone texting a mother, "Where are you? How much money are you spending?"

Officer Armijo had considered unlocking his bicycle from the trunk rack of his cruiser, but at the last minute decided against it. His balance isn't the strongest, and then there's his gun, and the cell phone which he'd used earlier to call an ambulance after he came upon a heap, facedown, on the sidewalk next to the Santuario. In a few minutes, he was able to gather the necessary information. It was breathing. It was a woman. Passed out on the cement below the feet of the Virgin de Guadalupe on the side facing the river. It could have been any one of his sisters-in-law. Now, he combs through the crowd on the plaza. Waiting. He needs to blow his nose but won't do it when he's on duty, making his rounds. It feels like a sign of weakness to him, a distraction that makes him vulnerable. He continues to wait. The tipping point is sure to present itself. The moment just before it all gets out of hand. How to know when it will happen? How to predict where? How to be ready? His fingers trace hat, badge, gun. He is in control.

Rufina's hands wilt. Which is to say, her drive has left her; the urgency for her brother's life is now eclipsed by her missing baby. Her foot keeping time on the tin is more of an accident than a commitment to rhythm.

Baby. Baby. Baby.

The angel reclines on a park bench, her boots propped up on the edge of a planter crowded with pink geraniums. She taps her heel on its edge. In her lap, her palms rest facing up. Empty. She's thinking about the children and their parents on the plaza, the balloons. The yearning. In the front pocket of her jean jacket, from the night before, Baby's two shells.

Rufina spots the angel on the bench, sees her staring into her hands as if reading them. She leaves the microphone, fisting her cane, pushing her way through the crowd. When she is among them, they no longer see how exotic she is. No longer see the fairy tale. They see the stains under her armpits, the dried skin flaking on her cheeks, the chipped polish on her nails, her limp, the cane. She is a waste of their time.

When Rafa sees a shadow, if he chooses to, if he concentrates, he can see what's there, waiting to be included: The lover sitting outside a hut in a strong wind. A snake coiled around her ankles. Or, perhaps, the healer riding a llama backward through a snowy orchard. He hasn't done this for years. Not since he tried to impress a potential boyfriend in Naples. His efforts were met with an explosion of insults. "You freak! You Latino faggots and your fucking magic. Reading shadows! Read my fucking asshole. Figlio di puttana!" The scowl on his love interest's face took some time to forget. The humiliation still pricks his skin.

The crowd in front of Rafa begins to scatter. He sees Rufina and the angel. Could he get the angel's attention? Could he manage something impressive? He steps up to the microphone, but is unsure of what to do next. The crowd stops dispersing and takes notice of him. He takes a wide stance. He will never be a man of any real height. On the ground, he sees a mess of figures, feathered, four- and two-legged, hooves, sees all kinds of weather, sees a river, a firepit, forests. He knows it won't be enough to call out the images he sees, if he can bring himself to focus. He'll have to do more. He'll have to convert the shadow arrangement into the question. The question, like a drawing salve, as Rosalinda would do.

As the crowd begins to disperse again, he locks on to the shadow of the couple closest to him and says, "It's too bad she won't let you touch her after dark anymore." The man he's speaking to wears a bolo tie with a Zia T-shirt. The woman tucks her thumbnail between her two front teeth. In her shadow, Rafa sees a child studded with raindrops sitting in a puddle.

"What the—" the husband says. "You talking to me?"

"You going to seduce her or not?" Rafa says.

"What the hell?" the husband says. "You're not talking—"

The woman says nothing. Curls her shoulders in; they slope toward her concave belly.

"You're not talking to me," the husband finishes. It's less of a statement and more of a string of words he seems to eat. They break apart on his tongue.

He turns to his wife. Pets between her shoulder blades, the place behind her heart, as if he's trying to wipe something off her. She turns her head away from him, then back. Clearly, they are both confused by this dose of directness. Clearly, it will take time.

For the next couple, in the man's shadow, Rafa sees a prince. Instead of a crown, a woodpecker stands on top of his head. Near him is a firepit, long cold; it's a pink-and-salmon-colored dawn. "When are you going to tell your father?" Rafa says. "About what you stole? Before he dies?"

"Come on now," the man says quickly, as if he'd just touched something too hot.

Strangely, the crowd leans in closer. They both want him to do it to them and don't want him to do it to them. They want to watch him do it to everyone else. Cut through. Expose. Money begins to drop into the basket.

Rafa is not invested in the questions he asks, or the couples. He doesn't care if he's right, if he's helping them or not. There's no feeling for him that goes along with it, just like when he performed as a boy. It's simply a game for him to play with his thoughts, pass time as he is watched, a way for him to invert the attention.

Officer Armijo notices Rafa at the microphone. Hears the collective gasping and sympathetic moans from the crowd. Knows this is where it will happen today. Feels the crowd churning. How close to a boil? Knows he will again use his phone, dispatch backup, but he hesitates. The last time he witnessed a sight like this was when Rosalinda stood on the ledge of the faux orno in the hotel lobby of the Dancing Sun Bear as if it were a stage. Nearly every guest had gathered as she called out the secret images, the questions that unraveled them. By the time she had finished and slipped out of the crowd, there were couples weeping, couples screaming, whole families on their knees, begging, wrestling, and pinning one another to the ground. He isn't close enough to know if Rafa is as good as the mother, but surely he learned it from her.

The couples in the crowd are now at the center. More passersby gather along the outer edges. They are transfixed. What will he say next? What will he divulge? Fistfuls of money land in the basket.

There is a cacophony of sounds. It is a tremendous, embarrassing time. When Rafa runs out of husbands and wives, he starts in on the teenagers who are coupled, then the mothers and daughters, fathers and sons, the pairs of friends. Never would he have imagined himself as a grown man without his mother in the plaza of his hometown, begging for money as if that would stop him from wanting to kill himself.

He is a kind of prophet-clown, a seer of what has tried so hard to remain unseen. It's as if he's entertaining the mother. He is fourteen, he is nine, he is three. He has learned how to keep her attention.

Five

○

"Why do you have to act like this?" Rufina says to the angel.

The angel looks past Rufina. Her wings twitch. "Like what?"

"Like a fucking kidnapper."

There are knots in the angel's hair; her headband is missing beads. The white leather beneath exposed. She looks at her watch:

1:49 pm
Sat. 5.30

"You've grown out of Baby."

"I have not," Rufina says. Rufina is on the verge of

kicking her one good, strong leg. As if she were a child again, the one who had been told that the baby who'd been growing inside her wasn't alive anymore, and that there would be nothing for her to keep, nothing for her to hold on to. And that the Explorer had gone and would never return. "Baby belongs to me. Baby will always belong to me."

When Rufina pushed, she forced another life into the world. There was the cord to cut. Baby not making a sound, Baby not breathing. Even though Baby's life returned to where it had come from, her hip had come undone and would never return to its proper placement. As she grew, the distance in her hip grew as well, forever a loose doorknob refusing to hold itself in place. Inside her, the wasted space for what was once there, promising life.

"You're not a mother," the angel says, slipping her long fingers into the band of her left sock, and then her right. "Baby didn't make it. You didn't birth life." She removes a half-smoked cherry Colt. "But you made it. You're still among the living."

Rufina struggles to push from her mind Baby between her legs, caught and wrapped by the Grandmothers to All. There was no crying out. No trembling in the light of the room and the cold air. She prefers it her own way. Baby placed on her chest. Baby feeding. Baby breathing.

"Speaking of mothers. What did you do with her? Did you hide her, too?"

As if on cue, there are mothers everywhere on the plaza. They walk in small packs with their children in various shapes and sizes. Their voices seem to fill the space with song, not unlike morning birds praising the sun.

Baby alive. Baby dead. Baby alive.

Mother alive. Mother dead. Mother alive.

Death was not a permanent condition when it came to those Rufina loved. Despite their hearts stopping, they still surrounded her, engaged her. And then there was Rafa.

"I'm not the only one who pretends," Rufina says.

"You're nothing like a woman." It's meant to be a surprise attack, but it's obvious and lacks the ability to puncture.

"Fair enough," the angel says, adjusting her crotch, unbothered. She touches her breasts. They're almost there.

Notice Rufina does not say, "I've had enough of you." Does not say, "You're a curse." Does not say, "What are you waiting for?" To say any of this would mean she'd be ignoring the angel's devotion to her for the past fourteen years. Her presence constant.

"Haven't you learned anything by having your prayers answered?" the angel says, hiccupping. Hiccupping happens only when the angel might cry.

Rufina remembers praying for a family, a father, her mother's steady attention, some kind of never-ending love. She prayed for the Explorer to return. She prayed for her baby to grow. She prayed for her mother to not be sick.

"I've been listening to you all along," the angel says.

"Have you?" Rufina says. "Listening to everything? All along? Or every other conversation? Or occasionally to requests?"

"Requests?" the angel asks.

"Please?" Rufina asks.

"Begging sessions," the angel says, finally, as if it were an answer to stop Rufina's expectations. "You, begging. Begging for everyone, anyone, to wholly dedicate themselves to you."

"You've never prevented anyone from being taken away."

"Since when was that a requirement for this experiment called living? Hmm? Being protected from loss?"

"You took away all my chances to have a family."

"The Explorer had to go. Your mother wanted it that way, and if you want to list someone's losses, try listing hers. That should make you feel better." The angel's ribs are visible through her T-shirt. She refuses to wear a bra. Clearly, her nipples are those of a man.

"He didn't know what happened to us," Rufina says.

"He did it, to both of you," the angel says. "Your mother got to choose."

"He loved us both. That's what he did. He loved us both but he didn't know we were pregnant. He couldn't have known. If he knew, he would've come back. I know he would've."

This was the force of Rufina's make-believe.

"Please," she says. "Don't take everything away. She didn't lose everything. She got to keep Rafa. She's always had Rafa."

"What they're doing doesn't concern you."

"How could that even be possible?"

"Stop pretending, Rufina," says the angel, whose hiccups have gotten away from her. Who, in this confronting Rufina, has become more upset than is reasonable for any being not of this earth. "Stop pretending that you could possibly know another's pain like you know your own. Your ability to feel for anyone else has been compromised by the restriction in your own heart, by your own wounding."

"That's not right."

"Then what is right, if not that?"

"I can feel everyone's pain because of mine."

"Brilliant. That sounds brilliant." The angel pauses. "But is it true?"

The pain in Rufina's body, the burning in her chest, which is not her lungs at all, but the inflammation of her own heart—this is what keeps her from answering. What does this condition actually provide? Restriction or potential?

"Are you going to let your brother win?" the angel says. She does not say, "At least you still have him." She does not say, "For a little while." There is what she will say and what she will not. The cigarillo between her fingers wags in the air, begging light. "Do you have a match?" The angel knows better. Nowhere on Rufina's person is such a thing.

"They'll return," Rufina says. "I won't be alone."

The angel searches the crowd. "What will return and where that leads—certainly that's cause for curiosity." When the angel spots Officer Armijo, she says to Rufina, "Now, there. Him."

Officer Armijo has trouble inserting himself among the tourists. He's pacing wide, trying to predict what Rafa's effect will be. The froth of the crowd seems to be settling. He can see Rafa's focus wavering. He keeps pausing and stuttering, throwing up his arms. He's not as talented as Rosalinda.

Rufina remembers sitting next to Lucio Armijo in seventh-grade homeroom. She remembers the pastillitos made from honey and the quince in his family's backyard, how happy it made him to have something to offer her. In eighth-grade homeroom, he brought her sopapillas with apricot-ginger jam, and then in ninth grade, handfuls of cherries. Always something to eat, as if she were a stray dog. He was convinced he could lure her with enough kindness and sweets.

"You want to ask him?" the angel says. "About his pain?" The angel is not devious, and yet. A man can love a woman and never touch her. A man can be more devoted to a woman who will never be his wife and save her in ways she will never know. Like this, every time Lucio Armijo thinks of her, he sees her in all her light, and guards that light, in his own mind. Even this can make Rufina safe, help her remember herself, ease the force of her shadow. This is not something the angel would be able to make Rufina understand. That the portraits in her room the night the Explorer abused her were not the only witnesses, that if she would've been able to see around the Explorer pressing himself into her, she would've seen Lucio in the panes of glass, watching. Unable to save her from a man easily twice his size and pale as unearned protection. Lucio will never leave his family and he will never not love Rufina with the whole of his aching heart. Which is to say, he has been trying to do anything to save everything, to atone for that one act he didn't commit. That night at her window, a conquest he couldn't find the courage to interrupt.

"You want to ask him what his pain has done?" the angel says.

Rufina glares. The hard point of her cane digs into the concrete of the sidewalk. She could do damage with that, as if it were the point of a high heel, the kind she has never been able to wear. She tilts it up as if aiming it at the angel's crotch.

"Suit yourself," the angel says. The cigarillo pops on its own, begins to smoke. The angel inhales until the red eye burns bright. The stink of artificial cherry pollutes the air.

"You're not being fair," Rufina says, returning the point of her cane to the ground with a whack.

"That's not meant to be a weapon," the angel says about the cane.

The angel grins. Her eyes appear glossy. She's about to tear. Her teeth are crowded in her mouth, tilting, chipped. "Your brother," she hiccups. How could she ever begin to explain fairness and divine chaos to Rufina? Death? Life? There never has, nor will there ever be, a language adequate enough.

"What are you planning?" Rufina says.

To those passing, Rufina and the angel appear as if actors in costumes rehearsing a scene. One is crying. One is about to cry.

"It's worthwhile practice, saying good-bye."

The angel exhales above Rufina's head. The smoke shifts about her, prayers lifting.

Six

◇

Meanwhile, on the other side of the plaza, because he isn't doing it properly, Rafa is drained by the act of reading shadows. His own shadow seethes with the residue from what he names in others. Because he isn't doing it properly, he gains in darkness. His own shadow doubles, triples in size. Flu-like symptoms begin to take hold. It's hard for him to distinguish between what he sees and what is actually before him. The light and the dark are becoming more difficult to tell apart. Projected images in the shadows and the concrete elements of reality around him merge. The softened edges of the adobe storefronts are muddled with the presence of snakes. Kings and queens huddle while pelted by hail. A hawk dives. Children follow parents, husbands follow wives, lovers meander hand in hand. Tourists follow vendors. Smoke clutters the air from unseen fires.

He's burping. There's bile in the back of his throat. He feels as if he'll soon vomit. The noise from the crowd is scrambled, side conversations, accusations, confessions. He sees a single hummingbird darting from shadow to shadow, piercing the edges of darkness, poking holes. He sees the people before him. Their bottom halves melting. Their mouths moving at impossible speeds.

Rafa feels himself funneled into memory. There's his mother saying, "Come play with me." It's an afternoon in late June and she's situated herself in the center of the living room floor. Papers spread out around her, small squares, not unlike a collage about to be constructed. She has soft-leaded pencils she's kept sharp by nicking the tips with a paring knife. A squat jar of black ink sits within her reach. Brushes stand at attention in a repurposed coffee can. Instead of settling down next to her, Rafa crawls out through the yard and into the garden. He's nearly ten years old, crawling instead of walking because he wanted to be a four-legged thing for the day. He wouldn't be a man for years, but he could be a beast, a powerful, powerful beast.

"Conejito, venga aqui," she called out to him. Three pencils of varying softness and a single sheet of paper waited for his return. Meanwhile, he growled and scuffed the soft dirt with his unharnessed strength. This was the world he was charging at. He burrowed his face into the plants, consuming whatever he wanted. He tore into the tender leaves of chard and arugula. Bit into the tart tomatoes still ripening. Once he had eaten enough, he continued chewing on everything he could find, marigolds, cucumbers, peppers, green onion shoots, the tendrils of weeds in between—all miniature and delicate. Then he spat it out. A wet, green slobbery mess trickled down his chin and arms. In between the narrow rows were the tracks of his hands and knees, as he had dragged them, his feet knocking over and bending the plants. The garden territory was a wasteland, wrecked. He was the beast that was capable of changing the world by exerting his force.

While the mother worked, she did not know what was happening to the vegetables she had planted. Did not know that as she stumbled through the darkness of her mind, creating ink and charcoal images, her garden was being ruined by the son who should've known better, but instead thought himself the most powerful force in the house, more powerful than the Explorer. Instead, she sat on the floor, sketching faces from the dark pools of her unconscious mind. Her imagination overrunning any evidence of memory. In the blanks in her mind, she renders what could have been. They were one and the same to her, what could have been and what was—remembering and imagining, imagining and remembering.

All of it real.

On the paper, the brush soaked with ink, whispering, not unlike the way the wind whispered, ancestors' voices hushed, in the dark beneath the banana leaves, hidden far from city lights, as the military approached her village, the smell of gardenias so thick in the air it seemed the cruelest thing of all.

Rafa continued to pull up seedlings. Peppers, garlic, and squash shoots, the fanning of new growth. He uprooted each one, and even after he grew bored of it, he continued in his destruction.

Now, in front of the crowd as Rafa throws up his arms, questions turn into accusations. He does not see loitering in the back, with his arms piled over his chest, a fifteen-year-old boy the size of a grown man. Does not see the way the boy's feet begin to move faster and faster until he is launching himself, missile-like, through the group despite his heft, aiming for a direct hit, Rafa's face. While this boy is unaccustomed to using his hands to do harm, once the first fist makes contact, he can't stop.

Squeeze. Aim. Strike. Release.

The force of his hand pushes into the surface of skin, stops at the stubbornness of bone. The quiet inside him is surprising and spreads down his legs. He knows where he begins and ends. The separation between victims in this moment is trigger thin.

Squeeze. Aim. Strike. Release.

His energy, endless. It was the last question Rafa hurled into the crowd that set him off. He didn't hear what Rafa had said just before, which was, "We seem to have an army of inept magicians lurking here with us today." He only heard the question "You ever get tired of being so pathetic?"

Rafa surrenders to the beating, relieved. His hat spins off his head, twirls away from him, tipping over the curb. The feathers flying loose. His knees aiming for his chest. His toes pointing. He's smiling. The fist coming at him, a blur; all the pairs of shoes stepping away from him, a blur; the shield of his own forearms, a blur; the mother cradling his head. Is that her voice now welling up in his ears?

When Rosalinda found him in her garden, curled nose to tail, belly bulging, she pinched him in the soft place under his arms. Flicked him in the nose with her thumb and forefinger as if he were a cat that had jumped onto the dinner table. Slapped the back of his head. She had gone out to smoke, to stand by the well, to stretch her neck and close her eyes at the sun when she made the discovery, her garden, him sprawled out in the middle of it. The carnage.

She tied his hands behind his back, which meant he couldn't flap them, which meant he was earthbound even in his pretend escape. This kind of behavior was something she would not tolerate. She had been betrayed. She wrapped her shawl around his waist and used it to fix him to the apple tree beside the well.

Throughout the rest of the afternoon, Rafa had visitors. The Explorer, who said, "Women like your mother can break anyone they please. Are you going to cry about it?" He waited for Rafa to cry and when Rafa did, he said, "There it is. Oh, little boy, you start crying about women now, you'll never stop for the whole of your godforsaken life. Leave her to me. I'm the kind of man who knows how to handle her." Rufina, who said, "You're a caca face," feeding him apple slices and dates. She gave him another name, Carnicito, and asked him if he wanted to be her pet. She scratched him under his chin and on his belly. "Where you'll have hair one day, you little beast," she'd said, just like she'd heard the mother say. All of this while Rafa's hands remained tied. No one was willing to interrupt Rosalinda's punishment and risk her turning on them, too.

It was dusk when the mother untied him. "Do you know how hard it is to survive?" she asked him. "If you knew, you wouldn't do such a thing." She carried him inside to her bed, where he lay in her arms. "Don't you ever do such a thing again." He clung to her. She clung to him. Their history together, as if hundreds of years old. All around them, the hills, mountains, and mesas bruising with the last light. The stars doing their best.

"You can't do that shit for money." Rufina is standing over him. There's nothing left of the crowd.

"I did it for you," Rafa says, his tongue fat in his mouth. He tries adjusting his vision. His right eye is swollen. He cannot locate the angel. "The money. Did you see the pile? You're winning."

"There's not a damn thing in the basket," Rufina says. "Not even the crystal."

He twists into himself. His face pulped. The world rings in one fractured note. His nose is not broken, but close. The mother is nowhere near.

Seven

◈

The teenage boy responsible for Rafa's face is not wearing his own shoes, but his older cousin's. He clomps down one street, and then another. His fist smoking. In his other hand the crystal. His chest a fantastic accordion. His eyeglasses are magnified and shaped like his favorite snack—moon pies. His joints are loose. Hidden like treasures beneath his flesh. Oversized clothes drape his soft body. His eyebrows tilt toward each other, his bottom lip droops. It's a permanent expression of misunderstanding, a mask of it he wears. He's hurrying as if he'll be left behind. He is always left behind. On his head, Rafa's hat. Under his right foot, snug in his shoe, the fold of bills.

He is not a boy, not anymore. With what he stole,

he could buy ink, just like his cousin. Down his neck, around his ears, down the outer seams of his arms and legs, around his wrists and ankles. Every prick of the needle will mean he exists. Has the right to exist.

I'm here, Cousin.

He imagines script fanning across his back. What does he have now? An X on the inside of his wrist, too small to see. A favor from the woman who marks his cousin. "Just getting you ready," she'd said.

Now he's convinced himself he's a man. Never mind how sloppy he is as he moves, as if each step lands in mud—no traction—and the effort walking takes causes onlookers to stare.

They see me, Cousin! I'm here!

A bandana wrapped tight around his head. The stems of his eyeglasses ride outside the material, pinching against the pattern of paisley. He wears navy scrub bottoms from the Goodwill. A gray oversized undershirt intended to show muscles, instead, tented over his body, revealing flaps of fat and skin. Look how hard he's trying. Rafa's hat, more shredded than it has ever been before.

As he passes by a pot of geraniums, he stops. They are not plastic like the ones at the cemetery, but alive, and purple-rimmed, striped. Candy on stems. A smile hijacks his face, his first of the day. A feral mess of lips, gums, and teeth. As if he's just gotten the joke. What does he know? Nothing. Which is what his cousin is always telling him.

I'll tell you what I know, Cousin.

It's his cousin he wanted to punch. Just this morning, in fact. After he skillfully scrambled the last of the eggs, his cousin swiped the plate from him as he was aiming his fork at the yellow sponge.

Cousin!

He heard the man at the microphone say, "Pathetic." It doesn't matter that the man was not talking to him, but to another teenage boy. "Pathetic, begging lump of a thing. I can't even make out what you might be." It doesn't matter that in his own shadow there is a sage, sleeping. He lies on the ground of a fallow field, a snake piled atop his chest, all of this dwarfed by a blood-red moon.

Squeeze. Aim. Strike. Release.

That's all he could manage. And as he was turning away, the money. All that cash. How the crystal ended up in his grasp, the hat on his head, he does not know. Never mind.

Look at me now!

Down Camino Agua Azul, then Doña Joya. He passes the tourists waiting in line at the corner restaurant. Then more geraniums. His smile at the sight of them. He stops at a two-story building of shops. Ducks under the exposed metal stairwell and steals a series of deep breaths. He removes his shoe, pulls out the fold.

Counts each five-dollar bill, seven; each one-dollar bill, nine; each ten-dollar bill, three; each twenty-dollar bill, twelve. All his now. He counts them again. Organizing them from greatest to least value. Folds them. Goes to return them to his shoe, and then there is the angel.

He slowly takes her in. Stares at her sideburns, the faint mustache, the chin hairs. He watches the rail of her body, the ladder-like quality of it. When finished, he says, "What are you supposed to be?" He has the faint memory of dreaming something like this once when he was a child sick with a fever. What's more likely, a homeless guy in a costume wanting some change.

"None of your business," she says. "Kid Thief."

"That's not my name," he says. He wonders if he can pick her up. Without thinking, he reaches out. She backs up with her spindly legs. He can feel the scrubby wisps of hair on her forearms under his thumbs as he attempts to lift. She is heavier than she looks.

An auntie with two children approaches the staircase they're blocking and maneuvers around. On the second floor is the local brewery and shops selling dream catchers and kachina dolls, a nail salon, and a smoke shop. The auntie holds the children's hands above their heads, steering them like puppets. Her cheeks crease as she smiles at the angel and the teenage boy. Lipstick marks her two front teeth. "Excuse us," she says, which sounds like she's making the noise of an oncoming train, a cartoon train.

"Cooz. Zah." Their progress upstairs is slow. The sound of their footsteps on metal stairs clinking as they rise.

"That's not your money," the angel says.

"Not yours, either."

"How much?"

He's already forgotten. Was it three hundred something, or four hundred something, or more?

The angel knows how hungry the Kid Thief is. She can feel his mouth salivating at the thought of a bag full of fried chicken tacos. She knows he will eat his weight. Feels the warm grease running down his chin like breast milk. He'll hold each one with his pinky up, stabbing the air as he takes each bite. He's already forgotten the fantasy of the tattoos. This one needs to eat.

"I can take it all," the angel says.

There's no way he can get around her. Or can he? He looks to the store window behind her selling tablecloths, napkins, and picnic baskets. The display makes him wonder for a moment what the insides of the homes look like, covered in all of that. He's not sure what a picnic basket is. A suitcase for rich people's kitchens? He smiles at his own joke. Thinks he is smart. Again, feels his hunger twisting.

Who said I wasn't smart, Cousin!

The auntie reappears, this time descending the stairs. Again, she steers one child in front of her and the other behind her. She has yet to let go of their hands. They each step down and then she steps. She will never let go of their hands. Which is to say, she is their guardian. Not their mother. Not their father. No actual blood relation. She is Auntie. The woman who stepped forward. The woman who cares. She is every woman in this place who cares, and they are all the children in this place. Know this—one day, in this place where they are all from, where they belong to someone, the children, grown, will take their turn leading her. After all, she is why they will never be discarded.

"Give me half or I'm taking all of it," the angel says, yawning. Her jaw pops. They both hear it. She wants to give him the chance to surrender the bills without force.

Women have a kind of authority he has trouble questioning, especially this one with her face like a woman's and at the same time a man's. The unexpected density of her. He's never sure what to trust. He squirms in his oversized shoes.

A gap has formed between them from where the auntie passed through with the children. The Kid Thief licks his lips. He feels the wad in his right shoe. His left foot stomps the ground in preparation, as if faking on the basketball court. But he is not on a basketball court, nor has he ever been, nor will he ever be. Just in his imagination, on the couch watching TV.

Watch this, Cousin!

Notice how the mass of him running causes everyone

to turn in his direction as he hauls west on Calle Chimayo. His fists cocked by his boobs. Before he makes it to Camino de Paz, he loses his right shoe, and the bills catch the afternoon air. They lift upward as if corn husk confetti. Through his thick lenses, he sees the angel three blocks down. She could be shaking her head. She could be flipping him off. Vision is a tricky thing. The bills continue lifting and whirling. People on the street, in the upstairs bar patio looking down on the world, think it's a cloud of trash.

The angel steps into an alley. Unseen, she calls the bills down to her pocket, as if they each had a name.

Eight

◊

Rufina raps the wagon's side with her cane. It pings. A sound Rafa cannot hear. Ping, ping, ping. It rolls toward her brother, stops against his back. As she stands over him, she longs for parents. She will always long for parents.

Rafa makes out his sister's shape. There is no angel. He's able to see what is clearly in the sunlight. All shadows are hidden, quiet. Rafa knows it was the boy with the body of a man who grabbed it. He's been beaten and robbed by a kid. The kind of kid he used to make fun of in his newly acquired French or Portuguese in the halls of junior high. This completes the insult.

Officer Armijo plants himself between the brother and sister. The husband and wife are there, too, suddenly, donation in hand, red-faced and out of breath.

"Go away," Rufina says.

"Nothing here for you to be an asshole about," Rafa says.

"Maybe it's for the best," Officer Armijo says. He shouldn't smile so much. "There's that problem with the permit. Not to mention someone could've gotten hurt."

"Right," Rafa says, holding his face.

"Apparently you don't have the same gift your mother did."

"You want my gift?" Rafa says, wiping blood into his hair.

"No, you keep it," Armijo says, "I'd hate for you to be any more desperate."

The wife has her billfold open. She claws at its contents. Considering what's happened, she's compelled to give them more. Two hundred from the ATM, as if freshly manufactured. She flags it above Rafa as if it will revive him, get him to stand up.

"They can't accept that," Lucio says, waving the wife away.

"Why not?" Rufina screams. "What choice do we have?" Her voice startles them all. The husband and wife step slowly aside before they turn and head toward the safety of their hotel. Their suitcases are already packed and standing upright next to the door. The alarms on their phones are set to the shuttle's pickup time. Once they have reached cruising altitude, the husband will press his hand on the wife's as if to flatten any upsets during their stay. When they're asked about their trip, they will both say it was the most fun they'd had in quite some time.

"Jesus fucking Christ, Lucio."

"Let me take you home," Lucio says.

It's the pain in her hip that makes her agree. The pain that is now piercing not only her hip, but the front of her groin and entire expanse of her lower back. It's affecting even her good leg, which thumps with an overwhelming ache.

Rafa won't look at either of them. He looks instead to the ground beside them. Shapes flush in their shadows, then disappear. Another wave of nausea. He uses Rufina's good leg to grip while he pulls himself up. "I don't want a ride in your circus car," he says to Lucio. "With your fucking lights." He grabs Rufina's elbow, hanging on to her, attempting to steer her away, but he's too weak. "He doesn't need to be at the house," he says in her ear. "I don't want him that close. There's no one there to rescue anymore."

All the windows in Lucio's cruiser are down. In the front seat, there is a computer between them fixed to a black plastic shelf that swings out from the dashboard, its beeps intermittent.

It's different sitting inside. The car's interior is gritty

and smells of stale coffee, sweet grass, and fresh, un-smoked tobacco. The seat is worn beneath her. She'd gotten used to watching it pull up the drive with Rosalinda in the passenger seat. She remembers the start of last fall, when there was water in the river. The air had been alive with the sound of water pulsing. She remembers breathing it in from the open window above the kitchen sink. Remembers the curtain pinned back. Remembers cutting corn off the cob. Remembers how food gave her mother stomachaches. It didn't matter that it was fresh. Everything gave her mother a stomachache. She was down to broths, a square of toast, a quarter of an avocado or sweet potato, mashed. "My body is eating me from the inside," she would say to Rufina as she lit another cigarette. "Stop putting food in front of me."

Rufina remembers Baby in the rebozo sniffing the air, peering at Rufina's mouth. Freeing a hand, the finger on Rufina's cheek, the fast strike of nail against her skin. Its hands on her neck like two paws. They were in the kitchen, making lunch. Rufina cut away corn kernels while she sang a song, which was a combination of several songs she misremembered. Songs the Explorer sang to her.

She stopped singing as she heard Lucio's patrol car parking in the drive.

"Not again," she'd said, wiping her sticky hands against her thighs.

"You're as miserable as everyone else," Rufina heard the mother shouting as she approached the front door. Rufina left the kitchen, headed down the hall. In her bedroom, she opened the trunk at the foot of her bed, tucked Baby inside.

"You can't pee in public," Lucio said. "She can't pee in public," he repeated when Rufina appeared at the door. "Not anywhere she feels like it. Not in the plaza, not in front of the tourists."

"I wasn't doing anything wrong."

"Again?" Rufina said.

This had been a problem for some time. As a young woman who had managed crossing borders on her feet, sometimes on her hands and knees, escaping a country that wanted all of her kind dead, and this while pregnant—a journey no one is meant to survive—had caused internal and external damage. Some of the scars were visible, others hidden. She was used to her organs doing as they needed. Which is to say, if Rosalinda had to pee, she peed. It was as simple as squatting and making sure her skirt was out of the way. She did it whenever, wherever she had to. Why should it have been any different?

"I had to go," the mother said.

"Why do you still do it?" Rufina said. "When you know you're not allowed?"

"I had to go."

"It has to stop," Officer Armijo said. There were rules. There was order. There were public bathrooms.

"It's not like it was in someone's house, on their floor," the mother said. "It's just on the dirt. The dirt doesn't care."

"Doesn't matter," Officer Armijo said. All the equipment suspended from his uniform lit up, his radio crackled.

"Ma, no one wants to see you peeing on the street."

"I can't have you doing it again," Officer Armijo said. "Rosalinda, I'm going to have to write you a ticket if you do it again."

"Write me a ticket? And then what? Put me in jail? Because I have to pee?"

"Ma, you're sick. You shouldn't even be out like that, alone."

"Call your brother," she told Rufina. "Call him right now." Every single time, it was Rufina who had to dial Rafa's number. The mother breaking down as soon as she heard his voice: "Conejito, mi amor, can you believe what they're going to do to me? Put me in prison! Because I have to pee."

Rafa came immediately, he always did. On the next flight from Paris, from Marrakesh, from São Paulo to soothe her. To protect her from distress. But this time he did not return to his life translating and traveling. He stayed and watched the exodus that breath made from her body. Five months later, it was complete. She was wrapped and carried out by the Grandmothers to All.

In the car, Rufina pulls her arms around her chest. She can't think of what to say but silence feels too much like death. "How's your litter?" she asks.

"Doing great," Armijo says. He adjusts his wedding band. Goes to trace his badge, stops himself. He sees his sons' faces in his mind. Eleven, eight, five, four. They resemble their mother more than they ever have him. He drives unbearably slow through town. Lingers at all the stops. Rolls away as if in neutral, as if uncertain of which direction he's heading, as if he hasn't delivered Rosalinda countless times to her front door.

"You sure you got enough of them?" Rafa says from the backseat. Spoken like a man who is not a father, who never will be. He's tapping the bridge of his nose and beneath his eyes. He has yet to see himself, measure the swelling, the marks, the impressive discoloration. The pain keeps him subdued, a more tolerable version of himself than he would otherwise be, contained like this in the back of Lucio's cop car.

"Actually, we're expecting," Lucio says, taking the curve up into the canyon at a crawl.

"Expecting what?" Rafa says. "Overpopulation?"

Rufina remembers her last day of school. Never again would they be their threesome, Rafa and Rufina, Lucio orbiting them. Her belly had grown too big to sit at the desks, just like a handful of other girls that year, as happened with a handful of girls every year at the high school in Ciudad de Tres Hermanas. The day came she quit showing up for class, and then Rafa left with a scholarship for the private school in the next town—he had impressed the school board with his dexterity with languages. It was the way in which he had learned to duel with the Explorer, compete for his mother's attention. They promised him college, internships, a life of constant international travel. Lucio Armijo went on to date and marry Candelaria Armijo, no relation, because that was always how it was meant to be. Ask any of Candelaria's aunties who had leaned in with all their weight during the courting season. They had four sons as if they were counting down to something, or counting up, neither of them can remember anymore. And here was about to be number five, another son.

Rufina's eyes are closed. The sun pools in the bowl of her lap, warming her hip. Quieting the raw, sharp sensation of the aggravated nerve. She listens for any sound of Baby. Tries to conjure all the places she didn't look that morning. Including the bed of the thirty-year-old Nissan pickup abandoned at the edge of the backyard. She pictures it in her mind. Her concentration is cut by the passing of traffic; the rock studded in the tread of the front tire clicking against the pavement. Again, the computer beeping.

As they round the next corner and climb farther into the canyon, Rafa begins shouting. Never mind the pain in his head, the nausea he's still burping from. He has spotted his hat and the one who stole it.

"No way! No way!" Rafa's voice is ricocheting off the interior of the car. "There's that fucking kid!" His own yelling is more than he can bear.

"He's the one that did that to your face?" Lucio asks.

"I know that hat," Rufina says. Her eyes are open now. Her vision sharp. She sees the soft young face of boy attached to the bulk of a man, tall and wide. Sees his braids, the bandana beneath the hat. His thick glasses melting down his face. His mouth is open. Everything about him seems to require space. Everything about him seems to be an apology for this requirement.

Armijo whoops his siren for a moment, turns on his light. There's no telling what the Kid Thief will do. But the mass of him is nothing short of a burden. His breathing is heaving; they can all see it.

Lucio reaches for his speaker, says, "You. There. Hold up." Then pulls over, puts the car in park. The Kid Thief does exactly as he is told.

Outside, a couple yards in front of the car, on the sidewalk next to the arroyo, under a demanding elm and tiny half-broken liquor bottles, the boy shifts forward and back as Lucio talks. Rafa and Rufina can't hear what they're saying. Rufina notices Lucio keeps his hands at his sides.

"He's telling that kid that he can give him a ride home. That he'll buy him a meal," Rafa says. "I bet you."

"How much was it?" Her chest is tight. She wants home. "Enough for a plane ticket?"

"Looked like it."

"How is it again that you cannot have any money?" Since her brother had left for college nearly a dozen years ago, Rufina had imagined him with multiple accounts all brimming with funds. Being in high demand as a translator for NGOs across the globe meant, to her, continuous income, endless opportunities.

"Goes fast." What Rafa is unwilling to admit, and always has been unwilling to admit: the investment he has made in lovers. "Mommy! Daddy!" one lover used to say to him after Rafa paid his rent, all his bills, filled his metro card, crowded his kitchen with food, his closet with clothes. There were the frequent trips home to Rosalinda, as well. Whenever she needed her son close to her, he appeared.

"Is that the crystal?" Rufina says, seeing it clearly in the Kid Thief's grip.

"Surprised he didn't take the basket, too."

As Lucio opens the back door, Rafa spits, "You're not going to put that back here with me."

"You're welcome," Officer Armijo says to Rafa as he guides the Kid Thief into the backseat.

Rafa swipes the hat off his head, dents it even further. He flinches as if Rafa's aiming to retaliate.

"Where is it all?" Rufina says.

"It, uh, it flew. Away."

"The fuck it did," Rufina says as Lucio eases back onto the road. The kid jumps at the volume in her voice. He's more afraid than any of them. His criminal behavior was out of character. The upward tilt of the expression on his face; the tip of his chin tilted down toward his throat; the way his shoulders are pitched so far up and forward all clearly state he's trying to shrink his mass. As they continue toward the house, he asks where they're taking him. He pushes up his glasses. His mouth hangs open. He waits for someone to answer him. When no one does, he leans toward the door. He's afraid of accidentally touching Rafa.

Rufina feels each stone under the cruiser's tires as it rolls up. The house appears tired, sad. She wonders how it looks to Lucio. If it's changed for him, too, now that the mother is gone.

Tulips dot the front and side lots. Multicolored mouths gaping, full throats revealed. The couch under the trees is soggy, the foam inside exposed. The porch is littered with candles all tucked inside colored glass jars. Scrap metal forged into stars and squares, moons and arrows rust against boulders and planks of wood. Old carved pews huddle around the firepit. Buckets of seeds and nails haphazardly placed. Beyond the house, the hills rise up to meet the mountains, beyond the mountains, the mesas. Everything crude and endearing as if made by hand.

"Nice place," the kid says, nodding in approval. "I like the painted parts." He's squinting through his glasses at the trim stenciled around the windows and doors. Vines, flowers, birds circling, trees expanding, a silhouette of the volcano—all of it appearing lush—and the monkey posing, as if the trickster, the deity no one has yet recognized. All of it is faded now. It had been the mother's work once the tiny stitches of hand sewing became too much effort. The house already knew what would happen next and soaked up the paint. Enjoyed the feeling of her hands— the stroke, the brush—as soon those same hands would be no more. It was a kind of therapy that kept her moving. Coat after coat, the mud surface of the house drank up the pigment and extended the time it took her to complete something that would stay and could clearly be seen. This was after she stopped wearing the costumes left by the Explorer, stopped loitering around town, stopped whispering to the wives, "Does he still taste as good as he used to?" And to the husbands, "Does she even notice you anymore?" This was after the countless times Officer Armijo had to escort her to his cruiser—more complaints of public indecency—and drive her home into the canyon where the quiet of earth and the embrace of the house would settle her down. "Ridiculous. Tourists. Not one of them wants to hear the truth."

"No one wants to be insulted," Lucio would say to her. For a time, it was a weekly event for the two of them, as if they were keeping an unspoken appointment.

"I'm sorry about your mother," Lucio says, turning off the engine.

"Not now," Rafa says. He tries to open the door, but it's locked. His fingers flip at the handle, a furious popping noise. Hot, sour liquid burns at the back of his throat. As if Lucio could relate to the mother, to what they were feeling.

"Irreplaceable." A generic sentiment and Lucio knows it. He means more but is unaccustomed to expressing himself. "Hard without her," he says, trying again.

"Open the door," Rafa says; he's feeling territorial, trapped.

"I don't remember my mother," the Kid Thief says. It's a quiet comment no one notices.

Then, louder, Rafa's mouth against the grill, "Let me out, cabrón!"

Rufina is barely there. She can hear Armijo and Rafa and the Kid Thief, a medley of men's voices. There's the trunk at the end of her bed and what she will not find. Her throat itches. She turns her head to the side, opening the funnel of her ear to catch all the hidden things. Hears nothing.

Officer Armijo goes around opening all the doors. The kid gets out as if it's his house, too.

"What are you doing?" Officer Armijo asks him.

He is at once a puppy, lost, his bulk deflating. Yes, where is it he has to go? Where did he think he was going? His stomach growls.

Cousin, he thinks. *Cousin, listen. It almost worked.*

Rafa's out and pacing. His face is bruised. It's a bruise that will spread and deepen in its shading until it covers half of his face, as if a birthmark, intense purple and red. His nose is swollen. Not broken but close. He pinches the remaining tips of feathers on his hat. Waits for something. Then lunges at the Kid Thief, grabbing the crystal out of his hand.

Two of the Grandmothers to All ride past. They ring bicycle bells once. Then break their pace. Stopping at the end of the drive, they watch and listen with their inner eyes and inner ears. They see the crumbling in Rafa's commitment to live—in his joints, in his spine—the young man's awkward shape, Lucio's fight to take care of them all.

Rufina is sipping air now. She knows what she will not find when she goes inside. She pulls her hair and thumps her stomach. Grinds her teeth. Thrashes. When her throat opens, it is a wailing that makes the men want to duck and cover. The Grandmothers to All hear Rufina's screaming and they know all that has been buried within her is so close to surfacing, will soon erupt. They begin to understand how severe the situation has become.

The mother did not tell Rufina it was her fault. She did not tell Rufina it was not her fault. She did not tell Rufina that she, too, was expecting a baby. She simply did not say anything to Rufina as Rufina's abdomen grew and grew and grew. Rufina has always thought that the mother asked the Grandmothers to All to search for the Explorer, to return him. The mother did no such thing. He never did return. Dead. Not dead. Dead. It was not discussed. The mother disappeared him. Then she disappeared what grew inside her, the start of a third child.

Lucio is wasted at the sight of her in his car. He's not sure how to comfort her, or if he should. Not with Rafa there, guarding her. Later, when he remembers this moment, he sees himself reaching for her. Sees himself carrying her to the house. Sees himself making it better.

The Kid Thief tears up. Turns his back. They all think they should be mourning what they've lost. For Rufina, it's the same and different. Mourning what could never be.

The hills look like strangers from this perspective

to the Kid Thief. Mountains. Beasts with their backs turned to him. He's never been this close. He can almost hear them breathing.

Armijo remembers his wife crying last month in the same way that Rufina is now, attacking him and the boys with her arsenal of pointed emotions. She didn't have anything left to give. The same thing happened to him then that was happening to him now. Any capacity of feeling, numb. His ability to feel his own pulse, gone. All of it frozen.

"Can you see her?" Rafa says, standing next to the passenger door. He thinks he can smell the mother. "Is she here now?"

Rufina will not move. The zipper on her dress has burst and there's a gash up the side of the material bearing her skin as if the dress refuses to hold her in anymore.

"Rufina," Rafa says, grabbing her cane. "Don't lie."

He bends down next to her. He is rubbing her arms and brushing back her hair with his palms. His sister isn't supposed to act like this. This is the mother's behavior. Rafa fights to hold back what he hasn't yet released. The whole, unending, consuming wave of it.

His touch reminds Rufina of Baby. She collapses.

"That's enough," he says. "Get out of the car." She is larger than him, and yet, he has a man's strength, which is enough. He pulls her up, stumbling the entire way, whispering into her ear, "Where is she? Tell me where she is." The Kid Thief shifts on his feet, makes an effort to follow, his hands out as if he can help somehow. They don't notice this. The house watches, though, knows how broken they are, takes them in.

"Hey," Armijo says to the Kid Thief. "Put your arms down. Get in the back."

Lucio Armijo watches Rafa shut the door, then, slowly as he can, drifts back to the cruiser. Helplessness threatening to drown him. The Grandmothers to All wait for him to drive by them.

"Looks troubling," one says to him.

He leans through the open window as if this will provide privacy from the Kid Thief in the backseat. "I've got a feeling," he starts to explain. "That something is coming." He goes for his badge but then instead grips the back of his head. He struggles with the ways in which he can know what is yet to be known. "And it's not good," he finishes.

The Grandmothers to All nod, each at their own pace.

"We're not far," one says, while the rest continue to nod. Which is to say they will return to the compound up to the road and prepare. They will be ready in the way only they, as women, can be. Ready for the unknown as it draws closer. Its presence in their bellies and hips. Sensations that will intensify. Life may be taken or given. Either way, their careful attention is required.

Nine

◆

On the way home, Officer Armijo stops at El Gallo y La Luna and buys a dozen chicken tacos for the Kid Thief. He could hear his stomach growling for miles. They sit at a picnic table next to a coyote fence, behind which run four lanes of traffic. Daffodils hug the fence line. They match the yellow wrapper of his tacos. He does not speak while he eats. His knuckles are shredded, open, raw. Nearby, a local couple wonders what the boy has done to be tagging along with an officer, wonders why it looks like he's getting a free meal.

Officer Armijo thinks of Rufina's wailing in the car. He can still hear it. His neck tightens. He remembers when she didn't have a cane. The way in which she stood was enough to win him over. He forever wanted to be standing next to that. Her gait, a move like nothing anyone else could do. He forever wanted to follow that. Her pace, that steady, slow swing of her hips, the call he forever wanted to respond to.

Rosalinda's voice is in Lucio's ears. As if she's next to him and they're sitting in the patrol car. The last time she was with him she'd asked, "How's your wife?"

"Fine," he'd replied.

"You sure?" She waited for him to tell her all the ways it was not fine.

"You're not fine," he said. "No reason to go to the bathroom like that in public unless you have no choice."

She stiffened.

"You sick?" he asked.

She ignored him. Instead, she'd said, "I've seen your wife's shadow. Seen yours, too. Poor in spirit, you. Poor in heart, her. But that could change with time."

Later, after he'd escorted Rosalinda to her door and kissed Rufina on the cheek, when he was once again at home and in bed facing his wife's back, he'd heard the echo of it, "fine." And he'd wished for his wife to roll over to face him, consider him something worthy of touching again. *Fine* meant what escaped him. *Fine* meant what was disappearing. The truth was sadder than he could contain. Instead of reaching out to his wife, touching that wall of her back, he'd scooped himself up, felt how small and soft he was in his own palm. Let himself drift closer toward dreaming.

After the kid throws away the last wrapper, he pats Armijo's arm as if he were Armijo's grandmother, like he knows how to console a man nearly twice his age. Says, "Thank you." Sighs. Says, "I can walk home from here."

Lucio wonders about Rafa's face, the missing permit, the missing money.

"You think I'm gonna let you go?" Armijo says, his mouth almost grinning. It's anyone's guess if he's serious. And if he is, about what, exactly.

The Kid Thief's mouth drops open. He tries to close it, but it won't stay shut. He adjusts his moon pie glasses. His lips glisten from the grease.

"I don't have it anymore," he says, trying to understand Armijo's expression, trying to understand the purchase of this meal, trying to understand what the *Officer* in Officer Armijo means. Tries to understand how afraid he should be.

"How come?" Armijo says.

"Wind came," the Kid Thief says, "and took it. Didn't matter how hard I was holding on."

"And."

"And," he says. "There was an angel."

"A what?" Officer Armijo knows exactly whom the

kid is referencing, and yet, he does not let on. He wants the money with Rufina. Now that he has seen, now that he knows her desperation.

Never mind that at this very moment the angel is lifting a rock at the base of the mulberry tree in front of the house, placing the fold of bills—which has been secured inside an empty package of smokes—beneath it.

"She, he—" The Kid Thief does not feel moved to tell the story of when he was six, when he was in the hospital, the fever, the angel he saw then at the foot of his bed.

"You assaulted a man," Officer Armijo says. He thinks of how close he once came to punching Rafa. Rufina's last day at school. Her stomach had been arousing suspicion for weeks. Everyone wanted to know whose it was.

"You wish," Rafa had said to Lucio. "Too slow."

"Oh," the kid says. "Yeah." He licks his lips, chews the bottom one, remembering the food he's just eaten. He sighs. "I didn't think I could—do that to someone else."

Officer Armijo knows the kid's cousin, and his cousin's girlfriend, and the woman that does his cousin's tattoos. He knew the kid's mother, too, before the overdose. The father, same. Keeping the peace. In the driveway, he wishes he would've picked up Rufina and carried her inside. He could have, easily.

"Be careful," he tells the Kid Thief, watching him stand. It's not the kid he means to say it to. It's everyone in the kid's life. It's the whole world that doesn't even notice him. It's the warden waiting at the Boy's Home on the south side of town, where the kid will end up in the next couple years because what choice will he have?

Armijo throws his legs over the bench, then walks the Kid Thief to the edge of the parking lot. Debates about whether to guide him across the street, as if he were only a toddler, pitching forward on incapable feet.

The Kid Thief adjusts his bandana and nods.

"What's your name?" Armijo says.

The Kid Thief hesitates as if he's forgotten his own name. He looks right and then left at the street, trying to gauge when to cross. "Alejandro," he says, finally.

The cars driving past drop their speed. One stops for the kid and then another stops. Soon, there is a row of cars on either side halting for him. He shuffles across the four lanes, looking toward the mountains. Makes his way down the unpaved shoulder, throws up a hand behind his head as if waving good-bye.

Ten

◈

There is no baby. There is no mother. In the canyon, in the house, Rufina is still in her ruined dress. She crashes around the kitchen, desperate.

Soon, she's breaking glasses, then the plates, then the ceramic bowls. Hurling them against the kitchen window, which shatters, against the counter, the walls. Throws all the tulip arrangements to the floor. The blue kitchen walls glisten as if imagining rain. The house shifts, sighs, holds her tighter.

"Fuck you," Rufina screams. She locates a bottle of mescal in the back of the pantry. Sucks down too much, too soon. It fires down the length of her midline.

"No matter what you do," Rufina says, addressing the angel, who is nowhere to be seen, "I can pretend it any way I want." As she swallows more mescal, her body surges with heat. Fire pulse. The whole of her burning. She continues to drink from the bottle. "I can make it so." There are two, then three of the objects in front of her, two canes, three couches, two hallways, three beds.

Rufina strips the sheets from her mattress. They catch around her ankles as she takes a step and turns. She falls forward, dragging herself to her closet, where she digs through the mess on the floor. She is a derailed force crashing again and again. She overturns all the drawers, opens the basket lid on her hamper; flips it up-side down. Crawls halfway under the bed and out again. Her uncles are hopeless in their portraits lining the wall. Their lips melted blobs, their eyes unfocused. So much black ink for the shadows around their mouths and down their necks. She throws the mescal bottle against the wall. It is a fantastic crash. The frames swing loose from their nails.

At last, she stands in front of the trunk at the foot of her bed, two trunks, three trunks, two trunks, three. Slowly grabs the top and lifts.

Nothing.

As she steps into the trunk, she collapses herself, pulls the top down. With it closed, her breath recircu-lates. She feels the rapid thumping of her heart. Scarves, Baby's pillows, the smell of alcohol. The force of her pulse, booming. Her hip a siren, wailing. All of her in need of rescue. She is in the trunk that was made in Spain, that traveled by ship, then by horse to a thick, wet overgrown jungle at the base of a volcano. This is what the Explorer had explained. He was the one who gave her this gift. As a girl, she would retreat inside, measure how long it took for someone to notice her absence, call for her, search for her. When they didn't, she'd emerge from it feeling at once the cool, fresh air about her, the light and the crisp audible sounds, as if she'd just been birthed. Later, on the plaza, for the Explorer's live installations, she'd stand on the trunk as tourists passed by and studied her, but didn't see her at all, throwing money in her direction.

She slides in and out of consciousness. The Explorer's hands are on her breasts, on top of her head, keeping her from inching away. In the trunk, among the scarves and Baby's pillows, Rufina's breath, heartbeat, and the smell of alcohol, suddenly is the angel. As if the trunk were a tiny boat and there, squeezed inside of it, they sit.

"There's not enough room," Rufina says. It had been the angel who bundled Baby, placed her in Rufina's arms. Saw to it that Rufina didn't die from the blood she lost. Stayed.

"But I'm in here, aren't I," the angel says. "With you." Her watch glows:

6:27 pm
Sat. 5.31

The smell of copal sticks to the back of Rufina's throat. The twigs of the angel's legs are pressing against Rufina's thighs.

"Tomorrow is Sunday," the angel says.

"I know," Rufina says.

"You have one day left."

"I know," Rufina says. "I'm the one who made the bet."

"How much money do you need?"

"What do you think?" Rufina says. "All of it."

"Things change," the angel attempts to explain. She does not mention anything about what is hiding under the rock at the base of the mulberry tree.

"There's not going to be enough, is there?"

"You're stronger than you can imagine."

"I'm not strong," Rufina says.

Rufina tries to turn her head. There is nowhere to turn it to. She lets her chin drop. Tries to shut out the angel.

"You're incredibly strong. You gave birth to a dead baby. You've endured."

"That doesn't feel like being strong. That doesn't feel like anything."

"See how easy being strong comes to you? You kept Baby alive all these years for yourself when everyone else knew better. You chose not to accept this loss. Even when you dug away the dirt beneath the mulberry tree while your own mother rocked in her chair on the roof. Rafa had comforted her instead. It was Lucio who was there, standing behind you in all his strength, as the dirt covered Baby, sealed Baby. The Grandmothers to All encircling you."

Rufina shakes her head. This is the way it had been, the memory lodged so thoroughly in her she'd nearly forgotten it. She'd meant to forget it. She'd done everything she could do to forget it. But there is Lucio. And the dirt marking her hands. And the circle of old women. The chanting. The smoke. She says to the angel, "I don't want to be strong; I want to be happy. If I'm happy I won't have to be strong." Her voice is not the voice of a woman. "I was happy when the Sotos came. I was happy when I was pregnant."

It's as if Rufina is not a grown woman at all. It's as if she's the girl she was before she started her cycle. The Explorer has not peeled her dress from her yet, while Rafa lay asleep in the mother's bed. She has not begun to swell, yet. Her stomach rounding and pushing skin. "I was happy when I wasn't alone."

"If you want to be happy—" the angel starts.

"We won't make enough for him to leave," Rufina interrupts. "If he stays, he'll die, and that will be my fault, too. I make everyone go."

"It's you who has to go," the angel says. "If you want to be happy." As she stands, she throws open the lid of the trunk. "You're going to need all your strength for that." Her wings unfold, springing up and out. She gives them a vigorous snap as if they were a sheet. "Happiness, you should know, is just another way of remembering who you are."

Rufina grips the sides of the trunk. The wood under her fingers has worn smoother than her own skin will ever be. Her hip is searing. "What?" she says. "What are you saying?" She doesn't know if she'll be able to stand. The mescal is wearing thin.

This is what happens when the angel tries to communicate—resistance, a barricade. She'll only make it worse, the harder she tries.

"Summon your strength," she says. "It is life coming for you. Your own future is coming for you, charging toward you with all its thundering force. Be ready."

Eleven

The Explorer was the kind of man who, after pulling into the drive that first time, got out of his car and followed the mother and her children inside the house. Even though, mind you, there was no official invitation. The house took note of this. This was one of the Explorer's attributes. He knew when to follow.

Once seated at the kitchen table, he began to take inventory of what was not there.

"No curtains. No paint. No dishes. No pottery. No record player. No plants."

Rosalinda, Rafa, and Rufina all looked around the kitchen and saw not what was there and had been there, but what had been missing all along. With the Explorer's naming of what was not there, everything seemed to be lacking. Where *were* the curtains? Why *didn't* they have paint on the walls?

Rosalinda had never felt so studied. Her veins seemed to swell in response. Her temperature became significantly warmer. She poured him a glass of water from the faucet. Placed it in front of him. When the Explorer's eyes paused from darting about the room, they landed on her. He was seeing her lack, too. That was obvious even if he wasn't calling it out. Rosalinda's heart rate was excessive. You should know that what she heard, in addition to the Explorer's listing of what was wrong, was the possibility of him making it right. In effect, what she heard was a list of promises. When the Explorer said "no paint," she heard that he would be the one to do the painting. That "no record player" meant he would be the one to locate such a thing, install it, and produce the records needed to fill the house with sound. In this way, she grew more and more excited as he continued with what was not there: sewing machine, rugs, candles, tapestries. Art!

He didn't leave once it became dark. They continued to sit around the table. Rafa on his mother's lap, Rufina the closest she'd been to reaching out and touching the large carved wooden cuff on the Explorer's wrist. Curiosity kept them pinned to their places. Who was this man? Where did he come from? What was he doing here?

Finally, the mother said, "If you're not going to leave, then you're going to need to sleep."

"I suppose," he said, his smile opening with all his bright teeth.

"Outside in the yard, there's a couch."

His smile turned loose. He nodded.

"Dreams are best sleeping out there," Rufina said.

"Don't tell," Rafa said. "He'll take them all."

"Will you?" Rufina asked. "Steal all the dreams?"

"I don't know how I could," the Explorer said. "When there are more than could ever be counted."

"That's not how it works," Rafa said, turning toward his mother. "Is it?"

Rosalinda did not respond. That the Explorer seemed to have appeared out of nowhere and had nowhere to go made Rosalinda feel a kinship with him. She was imagining the house filled with things, she was imagining him doing it. A man who could make things appear was a magician of sorts, after all, and she wasn't so burdened with her own devastations that she couldn't remember the possibility of magic, especially when it was seated across from her.

"Will you leave some dreams for us?" Rufina said, trying again.

The Explorer lifted the glass of water to his lips and emptied it without pause.

Later that first night, Rafa and Rufina watched the Explorer from the living room window. As he moved the couch so that it faced away from view of the house, and

managed a makeshift tent around it, Rufina bet Rafa that
the Explorer would never leave. Rafa bet Rufina that he'd
be gone as soon as the rains came. The betting continued.
Rufina—that their mother would fall in love with him.
Rafa—that their mother would chase him off with a machete. Rufina—that he'd become their father and they'd
be a family. Rafa—that the memory of the Explorer
would become so small that they'd step on it like a cock-
roach and forget he had ever existed. Isn't it something
how they both were wrong and they both were right?

The first week, the Explorer baked bread, collected wild
spinach and dandelion greens from the yard, and assem-
bled salads. With the strawberries he purchased at the
market, he made pies. Whipped cream with a fork until
it firmed, added powdered sugar and vanilla. Let Rufina
put her hands in the mixing bowl. All the cupboards
and drawers in the kitchen had been rearranged by the
end of the week. Utensils Rosalinda could not comprehend cluttered the drawers. Cloth napkins and towels
appeared, table linens, cutting boards, an assortment of
knives, pots and handmade dishes filled a glass-fronted
cabinet he'd put at the far end of the kitchen, along with
a sewing machine.

When he was through with the kitchen, he moved
to the dining room, then the living room, even the small

spaces at the front door and back door were filled with tiles and mirrors, milagros and cut flowers—irises, roses, daffodils, peonies. Rosalinda watched as he painted the walls deep tangerine, periwinkle, and mint. Clay pots bursting with herbs hearty as bushes multiplied in every room.

The house knew seduction. Knew very well this was what the Explorer was doing. And still the house sighed, still the house softened into a home for him, too.

By the end of the first month, the Explorer had begun to accessorize the mother. Just as he had done with the house, he selected items that matched his idea of her. Pink and turquoise dresses embroidered in red thread with blue and yellow hems. A red shawl embroidered with pink and purple thread. Everything embroidered. Saffron-colored scarves. Flowers in her hair, more flowers, more, until she was covered in roses and carnations, gardenias and mums. He propped her up in the dining room on a stool, a collection of small lamps surrounding her, arranged just so, as if she were a still life. He went through rolls of film when photographing her.

"Your people," he told her, the shutter clicking. "They could be from anywhere. Greece, India, Palestine, Bolivia, Polynesia. Such rich heritage." He had endless ideas about how to position her, how to frame her. Her beauty was dark and miniature. He loved the possibilities of her. To him she was a nugget of raw material waiting for him to shape, to mold into something far more exotic than she'd been able to create on her own.

As Rufina watched her mother and the Explorer, she noticed how the top of her mother's head reached the bottom of the Explorer's heart. She noticed that one of the Explorer's hands covered her mother's face completely. That when he put makeup on the mother, her features seemed to disappear beneath his movements. Undetected, Rufina watched how the Explorer would stand her mother on a chair, so they could be the same height. From this place, Rufina watched her mother gaze into the face of the Explorer. She imagined being placed on the chair, so she could stand eye to eye with him, too. And in the quiet of sleeping hours, Rufina would stand on that same chair, having got up on her own, trying to understand the sensation of height. Studying the room from that eye level, she glimpsed one of the benefits of this privilege.

"You know I'm here to stay," he told Rosalinda, kissing her dark-stained lips.

"You know I'll never leave you," he said as he hung earrings big as ornaments from her ears, placed rings, then more rings, on her fingers.

"You are the territory I've been in search of." He lifted her off the chair. Twirled her around.

It was his routine to cook for her, for all of them, with what he harvested from the garden. It was routine for him to wash their sheets, sweep the floors. He was their servant, of sorts, and in return they traded their human status for object status, to be conceptualized and arranged by him, put on display. In his servant role, he was hard to resist, and the mother surrendered to the force of his attention, she let herself hope.

After the first year, the Explorer relocated to the mother's bed. For the momentous event, Rafa stationed himself on the strongest branch of the mulberry tree next to the open window, flapping his arms as he listened to the Explorer moaning, "My muñeca."

What Rafa could not see was the Explorer's mouth engulfing his mother's ear. How very big his tongue was in comparison. The Explorer's mouth as it devoured his mother's lips. "Muñeca." How exciting it was for the Explorer to finally be permitted entry into her smallness, pushing past all of her resistance and numbness, as if finally filling a place that had been declared forbidden.

Rafa, in the tree, held his breath and flapped his arms even harder at the commotion. All the while, Rosalinda tensed. While his fingertips traced her forehead and the tip of her nose, she shook. The Explorer said he loved her. He loved her.

Rafa listened and imagined such a thing as love. Nearly eleven, Rafa convinced himself of what it was. Love was being an extension of another body, her body. Love was being ignored. Love was being severed, amputated. Love was being called back again and again. He knew love.

Outside, in the hall, Rufina brought the chair over and stood at her artificial height on the other side of the door, listening to the grunting and the moaning and the whining sounds that emanated. Her hands twirling in the air as if she were the conductor, not the Explorer, as if she were in command.

Over time, the Explorer's interest spilled over from the mother to Rufina. She'd been waiting for it. It was a kind of comfort to have her turn. He would sit at the table with her, books piled between them, candles on the countertops, his glass filled with wine, and show her the world page after page. For all that she did not know about who she was, he made known the possibilities. In those pages were histories and lands, stories and songs. She memorized these options of who she might be, where her mother might have come from, just as she memorized the way he touched her, his hands rough around the edges of his thumbs. The calluses of his palms catching in her hair. That was a kind of belonging, too, another way of being known. The delicacy of his attention. In this way, she was as important as the mother. Meanwhile, the walls and the rugs and the tapestries all screamed out loud and in color. Meanwhile, Rafa skirted the edges of rooms, watching his mother and his sister, waiting.

It wasn't long before the Explorer was dressing all of them. Had them staged in the dining room like an interlocking puzzle. After he dressed them, he told them how to stand. He pushed their arms and legs into place. Rafa would never hold still long enough. Hours they had to pretend they weren't real. It was a kind of rehearsal for what was to come. He had a series he was planning, instead of his mannequins, something much more compelling: live models. Something additionally exciting: new names. "It will help you forget who you were. Instead you'll just be who you are right now." He renamed them each weekend, depending on the country and the culture that inspired him. They knew which of them he was instructing based on whom he pointed at. This made the mother relax. There was no past. There was not even yesterday if she was no longer Rosalinda. All trauma momentarily lifted. With the trick of a new name, she could have been anyone.

"See how easy it is?" he asked. Only his name never changed.

It was common for Rafa to forget the new name he was given. "You'll always just be *conejito*," Rosalina told him.

"Try not to blink so much," the Explorer instructed. "Try not to do things like cough, sneeze, shift, sigh audibly. The trick is to make people wonder if you're real."

On the plaza, when tourist season was at its height, the basket splayed in front of them, they would make enough to last for months. The Explorer, nearby on a bench, watching, would later say, "What a beautiful display. What a masterpiece." The mother, beaming. "Look at her, everyone. Unmistakably beautiful. Rare and wonderful." Which is to say she was valuable, he'd made her so.

Twelve

◆

Shortly after the one-year anniversary of the Explorer's
arrival, the couple came to visit, Señor and Señora Soto.
They were friends of the Explorer's, or rather, they were
people he knew, which to him was the same thing. On
the evening they were expected, he stood at the counter
chopping celery, explaining who they were. He tried
to remember from the bar in Los Angeles what it was
they'd told him. Rosalinda perched on her stool. Rufina
sat at the table peeling the onion the Explorer would
chop next. Rafa was on his back, in the ditch next to the
road, willing snakes to cross over his legs, thinking about
the Explorer and how one day he would beat him at being a man.

"Can you imagine the electricity? They found each

other on the corner of Huerfanos and Banderas in downtown Santiago and ate each other raw for days," the Explorer began. "After all, they're Chileans." He paused,
considering what parts of their story to share. What the
Explorer did not disclose was they were Chileans whose
friends had been disappearing. Their apartments, their
pets, their cars—sometimes still left running, parked
along the street—anticipated their return at any moment. Nor did he disclose that they were coming because
they were afraid for their lives, that they were running.
From what Rosalinda would not tell him, he'd gathered
her immigration experience was much different. She'd
not been able to buy an airplane ticket, then upon arriv-
ing in the States, purchase a car which she could drive
from city to city until she found something that might
suit her. From what Rosalinda would not tell him, he'd
gathered she had to crawl her way out and that what
she'd endured while doing so left her unable to state simply where her village was, what was the closest city, what
the country was called, exactly, after all, she'd once said
all these things in her language, which refused to be re-
routed to Spanish, to English.

On the record player, Amália Rodrigues. The Explorer switched from the celery to peeling hard-boiled
eggs. He was making egg salad for dinner. "Oh, how I
wish I were Portuguese," he sang, interrupting the start
of his own story. The apron he wore, covered in eggplants,

hid his shorts. The material had been on sale. Rosalinda had made it for him. It looked like he was wearing a dress. Somehow this amusement made him seem less tall, less white. She appreciated this, too.

The Explorer considered Rosalinda's lacking information as if it were a secret. This made more sense to him, as he had his. His secret was this: He was from the south, from the hills of North Carolina. His ancestors from Scotland or Ireland or England. But with Rosalinda, and the children, he could pretend himself to be so much more. He did not have an accent, that troublesome southern twang. And because he had read so many library books, and had listened to the programs on the radio, and knew all the worldly, cultured things that worldly, cultured people knew, he liked to imagine himself altogether different. While he did not actually travel abroad, he mined his international acquaintances for all the details he needed to create an alternate reality where he was a man who traveled the world. He was a man of ideas, who learned to speak in a variety of languages. He was far from where he originated, his mother in her housecoat with drugstore wine on the davenport, his father a hired hand in someone else's field. All of his towheaded brothers and sisters like used tin cans tied to the tailpipe of a car, bouncing off one another, making as much noise as they could. He was different. He was an artist, and his most impressive creation was his own identity.

The Explorer turned up the volume on the record player. It was wailing and it inspired Rafa to return to the house, to the kitchen table. Rufina sang along. It was the screaming of it that thrilled her.

The Explorer winked at Rufina. Did he wink at Rufina? He meant not to wink at her. She was so easy to play with, to tease, to flirt with. Her sweetness in perfect measure to her wilding. The surprise of her at any moment. He'd been drinking since ten that morning, since last year, since he was thirteen. Big, tart wines that turned him into a raft of flesh, carried him out and away. Quite often he found himself to be in deep waters with no land in sight. When he was in this state, it was as if he were a boy. Searching. Searching to find his mother and tell her how pretty she was. Searching for his mother, who would share with him from her cup. She is drunk. He is drunk. She is happy. He is happy. He is loved.

Rufina handed him the onion and the Explorer was back in the kitchen with Rosalinda, Rafa, and Rufina. Singing at full volume, he placed a glass bowl of chocolate pudding into the top shelf of the refrigerator. At the door, a woman appeared. Her skin was opal, and beneath, on her chest where her lace blouse was cut away, a network of veins made visible.

"Buen dia," she said, blushing, blotches of uneven crimson marking her face, multiple strands of yellow beads wound around her neck. Tall and flat, she was void of curves from any angle. Her hair was pale and flat, too, as if the whole of her were run through an industrial-sized pressing iron. Her bangs plastered to her forehead, two tight braids, pulled into a twisted crown. Rufina couldn't look away. Blanca Soto. The husband behind her was opposite in appearance, dark and short and round, with bulging black eyes and loops of tight black curls springing from his head. Paulo Soto.

"These are my friends," the Explorer said, pointing to the husband and wife as if convincing everyone in the room, including himself.

"Children!" the couple seemed to say in unison. "Children!"

"You didn't mention there were children!" Blanca said.

"Hello, children," Paulo said. "Beauties," he whispered to himself, his eyes moist.

"Tell us your names," Blanca said, kneeling on the floor.

Rafa and Rufina responded quietly from the opposite side of the kitchen where they'd huddled next to the fridge in an attempt to grab the pudding when the Explorer took swigs from his wine.

"Please, come closer," Blanca said. She held out her hands. "Just look at you, Rufina. Are you the youngest?"

Rufina nodded.

Blanca embraced her as soon as she was close enough.

It was a move that Rufina wasn't sure how to engage. As she considered her options, she felt Blanca's heartbeat, the skin on her arms, her neck, her face, cool. She didn't know what it was to have an aunt, but she imagined this might be it. She expected Blanca to release her but instead, Blanca continued to hold her. What the couple knew but would not speak: three weeks prior, in Santiago, Paulo's pregnant cousin and her husband had disappeared. It would have been the first child on either side of the family. Since then, they wanted to hold every child they saw, but that, of course, had not been possible. At last, in this moment, this house, there was Rafa. There was Rufina.

"Beautiful, beautiful girl," she said. "How lucky is your mother to have you."

And in that moment, Rufina felt Blanca's words, it was a new idea—to be beautiful, for Rosalinda to be lucky because of *her*.

Paulo wiped his eyes. Turning to Rafa, he said, "Compadre, you know how to play the guitar?"

Rafa shook his head. "Never touched one," he said.

"I just happen to have a guitar in the car that would love to be played." He extended his arms, which was an invitation for Rafa to climb into them.

Rafa hesitated, looked at his mother, stepped one set of toes and then the other set closer to Paulo.

"I'll teach you a song. Yeah? I'll teach you the best song

I know." It was obvious to everyone how hard Blanca and Paulo were trying, and it was also excused. Their longing clearly felt by all.

Rafa got close enough for Paulo to lift him onto his back. "Let's see what else we can find out there in that car. Some fun stuff, compadre, I'll tell you that. You just wait."

Rafa was not sure what to make of riding on this man's back. He was not a large man. Nowhere near the size of the Explorer, to whom Rafa had never been this close. But he was strong, and he cried, and he giggled, and he looked at Rafa like he was the prince soon to inherit the throne.

Dinner was served on sandwiches without crusts along with sliced golden beets and warm, soft cheese. Rosalinda, Rafa, and Rufina watched as the Explorer and the Sotos drank bottle after bottle of wine that the couple seemed to have stored, among many other belongings, in the trunk of their car. Blanca made every attempt to express to Rosalinda how perfect her daughter was, to which Rosalinda responded by taking another drag from her cigarette. Which is not to say she did not love her daughter, because she did, but she loved her differently.

✦

Later that evening, they all agreed to take a walk. Rufina donned her animal mask. It was a badger, or a squirrel, or a rat. Blanca and Paulo took turns wearing it, then placed it back on Rufina's face. They growled and screeched and squealed together. Rufina's feet did not touch the ground, Blanca and Paulo carrying her between them. Rosalinda drifted behind, pretending to be distracted by the hollyhocks and the lizards shooting across the road. The couple's easy nature and full expression of adoration gave Rosalinda a terrible headache.

Rafa investigated the wife, her thin bleached hair, the shadows under her eyes, her thin pale lips, the plank of her body—she didn't even look like she could chew meat let alone travel across continents. He curled up against his mother. Put his nose against her chest, tucked it under her arm, inhaled.

Rosalinda could hear Rufina's voice, how loud it was, the way it carried. Rufina's voice upset her. When she was upset, she became panicked. When panicked, the contours of a face appeared. Soon there were boots marching, voices shouting, the shrill slicing of screams. The explosion of blood in her veins.

"Quiet!" she shouted.

Up the road, Rufina heard her mother and knew it was meant for her. She ignored it, howling as loud as she could.

"Quiet!" Rosalinda shouted again.

Rafa ran up ahead to carry her message.

The wind in the trees gained momentum. Lightning streaked the sky, and soon thereafter, the thunder. Blanca and Paulo joined in, increasing the volume of animal voices.

"Now monkeys!" Blanca said.

"Now wolves!" Paulo said.

"Now cheetahs!" Rufina said, and they rivaled the noise of the descending storm while all around the insects rattled and trilled as if they, too, were frantic with forgetting.

"Quiet!" Rosalinda tried one last time although no one could hear her.

"You're being too loud," Rafa told Rufina and the Sotos. "You're hurting her."

"How can that be?" Paulo said.

Rufina had already begun deflating at the notion of hurting her mother. "She hurts in ways we can't understand. That's what she tells us," Rufina explained to the Sotos.

"You always have to make it worse," Rafa said.

"Does she tell you the stories of how she came to hurt?" Blanca said, kneeling on the pavement to look Rufina in the eyes.

Rufina exchanged a look with Rafa.

"No," he said. "There's nothing left to remember."

"She gets dizzy. Then she screams. Next, she'll cry

and mumble those words, lock herself in her room," Rufina said. "That just what she does."

"When she hurts?" Blanca said.

"All the time," Rufina said.

"Rufina!" Rafa said. "You're not helping. She doesn't want us—We just need to comfort her better."

Another torment of thunder, again the streaks of lightning. It was nearly dark. The Explorer, far ahead, was not cognizant of the distance his long stride had taken him. He gripped his wineglass, which he'd carried with him, as a new understanding threatened to take root in him. In that moment, he began to feel how it did not matter how many books he'd read, or films he'd seen, or languages he'd taught himself, or how much he'd struggled to contain the world in his installation art. The cells in his body would never comprehend what it meant to be violated by his own country, to have to give it up entirely, to never once return to it. He drank from his glass, a kind of gulping like he did as a boy.

Fifty feet behind him, Rafa attempted to explain to the couple, "Really bad stuff happened to her. You wouldn't understand."

"Do you understand?" Paulo said.

"No one can understand," Rufina said. "That's what she tells us."

"I'm walking her back," Rafa said, changing direction. Rosalinda had stopped and was staring at her tracks on the road. As he approached his mother, he held out his hand for her to hold.

It seemed as though hardly any time had passed before it started to rain. Large, heavy drops with considerable pauses in between, then the downpour. They all were drenched by the time they reached the house. The power had gone out and Rafa continued holding his mother's hand in the dark. Blanca held Rufina while Paulo flicked at Rosalinda's lighter as he searched for the candles. By the time the Explorer returned, the house was glowing as if it were a lantern.

"She can't stand this darkness," the Explorer said as he picked up Rosalinda. "Not when she can't control it." He took her to her bedroom. They all heard the door shut.

"How about some dry clothes?" Blanca asked the children. "As fast as you can, and when you're done come back to the kitchen and we'll melt chocolate to drink. How's that?"

Rafa was back first without a shirt and wearing a pair of sweatpants that were too short. His damp hair spiked in all directions. Rufina wore one of her performance dresses, which received applause from the Sotos. Blanca brushed Rufina's hair and braided it while Paulo melted chocolate on the stove. They topped it with cream and sipped it while he sang for them. "Return. Never again, return. *Con todo mi anhelo. Con todo mi vida. Vuelvo. No volver.*"

✦

Rosalinda stayed in her room for the week. She smoked her cigarettes, the incense lit. Her bed, a sanctuary. The Explorer served her food on trays. The Sotos took Rafa and Rufina for long drives in the country, Blanca telling them, "Once upon a time there was a little boy and a little girl who lived in a canyon with their beautiful mother, who was *muy afligida* . . ." And as they went for Frito pies and ice cream, cheeseburgers and sopapillas, Blanca repeated and continued her telling. "Both the little boy and the little girl were magic, decorating the mother with their constant love. They were special children, loyal to their mother and her pain, only wanting to help her, the boy with his strong arms and heart, his laughter, the girl with her strong spirit and her beauty, her gift of casting spells. But what the little boy and little girl did not know, what they could not imagine . . ." And as they went to the movies in the theater downtown, they sat on Blanca's and Paulo's laps with their hands in popcorn, snuggled like all girls and boys should be. Then, the strolling through streets playing "I spy," until every inch of Ciudad de Tres Hermanas had been touched by their eyes. Blanca continued her telling as if it were a chant that might protect them long after she had gone—"The mother could not care for them like they cared for her. And one day they would have to choose to stay by her side, or turn away from her, and follow their own magic into unknown lands and onto adventures of their own where monsters and angels alike waited . . ." Paulo never spoke while Blanca doused them with this story. After all, he was counting down the days until they would return to Chile and be reunited. Even though that day would never come. Still, he stayed quiet, didn't embellish it in ways it could have been. Instead, he listened, too, as Blanca got to the end of her tale and began again. He knew what she was going for: presenting a story to the children where they were at the center, not the mother, would perhaps awaken their own life's possibilities. That his wife was doing this made him love her even more. And at the end of the last telling she would ever give, Paulo asked them, "What will happen on your adventure?" To which Rafa replied that he'd turn the mother into a lizard and keep her in his pocket as he sailed all the seas there were. While Rufina said that in her adventure, "The sun will fall in love with me and we will fly away together."

On the evening Rosalinda finally emerged from her room, light drained from the sky, something ordinary had happened, which is to say none of them could undo it, which is to say the darkness would soon do what only it knew how to do, cover and conceal, while the stars made their attempt to poke holes.

Meanwhile, Blanca and Paulo stood at the end of the drive arguing about the mother. Paulo called her a tragedy. Blanca called her misunderstood. They continued to argue as they got in their car and drove away, having not said good-bye to anyone. Something they couldn't bring themselves to do.

Meanwhile, Rufina brushed her hair, twirling in her room, twirling and twirling, fueled by a joy she'd never felt like this. It was years before the baby came to be as Rufina imagined a mother's love, a father's love, imagined an entire family with her at the center as she twirled and twirled remembering Paulo's song, remembering Blanca's hands in her hair, remembering the sweets on her tongue, considering herself as Blanca insisted, as the thing that brought luck to others. The story Blanca told her falling deep into her being, not unlike a seed.

Thirteen

On the other side of the door, Rufina is calling down to Rafa at the bottom of his pit. Any presence he'd had earlier that day on the plaza, any emotional thrust, any investment for living has now gone. Frankincense burns. Golden crumbs of it on hot coals on the shelf above the mother's bed. A fog of it in the room. Rufina can smell it from under the door. The mescal is nothing like it was hours ago. The mother's door is locked, and Rufina rattles the knob. She studies the hinges, goes to search for the best tool to undo them.

The mother's bedroom was never a place for Rufina. Unless she wanted to pick at the calluses on her mother's feet. Unless she wanted to massage oil into her mother's scalp, or rub lotion onto the mother's legs, legs that continued to seize up with the memory of her journey, thousands of miles, one punishing day after another. Being pinned down—soldiers, rebels—men's faces, blurring, too close. How could she tell which they were? The dried blood on their hands. Bits of chewed meat passing from their mouth to hers, making her gag, her stomach growling, the forced opening of the raw wound between her legs, the deeper cut. The way it happened was exactly like she'd been warned. The rebels had been caught in a surprise attack. The soldiers sprayed bullets into the dark. In that moment, she crawled away, heading north, the volcano a massive silhouette behind her. The only divine presence she'd ever known. Skeletons running. Mountains shifting. She would need a way to find herself as all she knew emptied out of her.

What she remembers: Night. The blinding force of a flashlight. Hands pulling her along. A blanket. Women's voices. The open trunk of a car. The final border. Being caught. Being wrapped.

For days, the Grandmothers to All had acted as her own hands, feeding her, bathing her, helping her drink the tea that would protect her from nightmares, giving her phrases to say in English, placing each word on her tongue. They had visited her daily, paused from the work of bees and harvest, from writing letters to the government of El Salvador, to the government of Honduras, to the government of Guatemala, letters to the president, to their representatives, to the governor, to the mayor. They were plain women, militant about their causes, sovereign as dirt. They taught the mother to read and write, but she preferred to draw, to paint the faces that flashed through her mind, catching what was familiar. They lent her the house, because the house existed for such a thing, for someone who had been forced to flee, for someone who suffered the holy humiliation of having made it, of being termed a "sole survivor." The house was less than a quarter mile from their compound and it kept her safe, it tucked her in, it sang her to sleep, it kept watch. She had just turned seventeen, and then there was a baby, Rafa, a reason to live.

In the end, everyone faded from her view, eclipsed by the fighters surrounding her. Instead of machetes, they held bouquets of sword lilies. Deep red flowers full of life and blood and heart. What is cancer if not a malfunction of time? Centuries compressed inside her, the rapid mutation of cells crystalizing. All those ancestors, begging to be counted, calling out. Her bones went porous. Filled with air and light.

She'd been dead four months, or sixteen weeks, or one hundred and twelve days, or two thousand six hundred and eighty-eight hours. Nearly the same number as the miles she had covered once, while her son grew inside her. Now, there he is on the floor. A man sprawled out as if exposed on the battlefield. She senses the possibility of letting go as it blooms inside him. He will feel the beginning of it, a simultaneous sinking-and-lifting sensation, and then be overtaken by the relief.

Know this: The mother had read the Explorer's shadow on that first day she met him in the sewing shop with no name and saw everything she needed to. She could've asked him, "Will you choose to hurt or to heal?" She could've asked him, "What will you do with your pain?" Seeing into his shadow didn't make her able to read the future. If he was going to hurt her, she didn't know how, to what extent. For now, she's still submerged in the well where the angel put her. Waiting.

And about shadow reading, there's no way you could know how old this capability is, how ancient the art form. The original images go back before any royalty, back to when animals had their say, back to when even the creatures in the unseen realm could permeate the veil. It was a way for the spirits to intercede, a way for the people to correct one another without weapons, a way to sense into and beyond. What Rafa did in the plaza was a drop from the lake of this knowing, the smallest of expressions. All it did was defeat him, exhaust him. No one present benefitted. There was no medicine of observation or questioning dispensed.

At this hour, one town to the north, far from any tourist, is a trailer in a lot at the end of a dirt road. Inside, Alejandro, the Kid Thief, lies on the couch watching the TV blaze in the dark. His stomach growls. His cousin is passed out with his girlfriend in the back bedroom, having cashed in their food stamps for caballo. Alejandro's hand is still swollen and split from the punch he delivered to Rafa's face.

Rufina gives up on trying to take the hinges from the door of her mother's room, something the house refuses to let her do. Her brother has gone quiet on the other side. Now, she goes through the rooms collecting the broken dishes. With all the pieces, she sets the kitchen table. She can see Paulo and Blanca Soto, Rafa, too. They'll sit down together and eat roast chicken with strawberry shortcake as if children with parents, as if family. Blanca will ask them what they would like to dream when they sleep. She will say that their dreams are listening and that their dreams will come and find them even when they are lost. Which is to say, there is no need for you to lose heart, not yet.

The angel knows that the rope attached to the well is no longer there. That it is coiled, not unlike a venomous snake, under the mother's bed. There is only so much the angel can do.

Sunday

One

◆

Sunday, late afternoon on the plaza, and the tourists present are sparse. They speed-walk to shuttle vans, wheeling their suitcases behind them, bent forward as if mimicking the planes' ascent. They are unsure if they have the correct time for their flight. They check the apps on their phones again and again, calculate time zones, minutes to the airport, bags wagging behind like tails. Those who remain rush through the streets, attempt to grab that last souvenir, attempt to memorize what's before them as if they'll never return. As if Ciudad de Tres Hermanas will disappear once they've gone, no longer in existence without their presence.

Rafa has a rattle. He shakes it now and then as he stares up into the tops of the cottonwoods and box elders. Considers the crows. He's still in the same clothes. Well, he's still in the same pants. The vest is gone. He's bare-chested and bare-footed. Not changing his pants in three days means they've stretched out beyond their size and hang from his hip bones, reeking. Even in this state, he's attractive; a kind of animal-like musk still causes people to slow and look again. Take him in. He'd promised his sister the whole of the weekend. This is the last of it.

Rufina beats a hand drum and wails. She's wearing a blush-colored slip with shells sewn onto it. There are her unshaven armpits. Her one leg stronger than the other. Her cane on the ground in front of her like a line no one is permitted to cross.

Everything is exactly the same as it has always been on the plaza. The laborers shuffle from job to job, still trying to make Mass. The Original Enduring Ones survey the scene, predict the day's sales.

A group of white women in their fifties or sixties or seventies tour the Southwest without their husbands. They parade around the plaza. With each lap, they gather more courage to start a conversation with one of the sellers.

They delegate a leader. The leader picks a man at the end of the row of sellers. They huddle around him. She asks, "Now then, what tribe are you?" Her name is Betsy or Susie or Patricia. She is unaware of the demand in her question, the exhaustion her privilege causes in those without it.

He does not want to tell her. He does not want to hear who he is come out of her mouth. He does not want to have to correct her pronunciation.

He is so pretty, she thinks but will not say until later, when the women are traveling home, congratulating themselves on another adventure. And then she'll say, "And wasn't he just so very pretty?" She wears a squash-blossom necklace like his grandmother's. Something he would never be able to afford if it weren't already in his family. He names the pueblo he is from. Gives the Spanish name instead of the actual name. "Oh!" she says. "I was just reading about all of you." He is thinking about his new wife and how when he crosses the threshold to their home, she is there to welcome him in their language and how this is the medicine that keeps him from feeling like he's selling part of himself when he sits all day, every day, negotiating the price of his hand-pinched pots.

The woman in the necklace explains to her friends everything she knows about who she thinks him to be. Once she has run out information, she grunts.

"Now you talk," she says. Her eyes are loaded and bearing down on him. The women are in junior high again, surrounding her. They are impressed with her knowledge.

He grins. He is the Navajo man, or the Zuni man,

or the Hopi man, grinning. Grinning is what he's become accustomed to doing when insulted. Says, "Close enough. Smart woman. Close enough."

He's willing to tolerate them for a sale. They could easily fund his expenses for the next few weeks. The women, however, are more pleased with themselves than with him. When he doesn't add to their narrative, provide an impromptu history lesson, they wander off. Hunt for other entertainment.

The women wanted a conversation! They wanted him to make them laugh!

He'll have to explain the loss of this income to his wife. And during the ceremony, when all living things are acknowledged and thanked, protected and blessed, he will remember these women and they will have no idea they are being considered, prayed for. As they lap the plaza again, precious as a flock of guinea hens, they pause by businessmen gathered in front of Rafa and Rufina.

"Well, look at that . . ." the leader says to her friends. "What would you call that?"

"Odd," says one.

"Surprising," says another.

The men in suits and ties clap for Rufina. They sparkle and shine. Their wedding bands glisten on their fingers. Slicked-back hair and leather shoes, gleaming. Squeaky clean behind their ears. Flossed teeth. High-SPF lip balm shimmering in the sun. How fine they appear, effortless in their pride, and yet, there are shadows—you can imagine—the hunger that will not stop no matter how large their bonuses. They are from Chicago or Miami or Phoenix.

Rufina refuses to acknowledge the pack of them.

One of the men, whose name is Kenneth or William or Richard, spots the cane. Points it out to another man in a suit, who points it out to another, until they all are aware of its presence. There is mumbling under breath. Heads are cocked and the backs of hands held up in front of mouths to screen what is being spoken. There is a kissing noise. The youngest man, Austin or Stewart or Jacob, is blowing Rufina kisses.

Still, she will not look their way. She feels as if her head is in a rusted tin can at the bottom of the arroyo, her body, her breath an intolerable nuisance.

Without any more dramatic gestures, or goading—and as if in unison—each of the fifteen men withdraws his wallet. It seems like a choreographed move. The flip of the suit jacket without looking, first one and then another and then another, reaching for and then locating the leather. Know this: Last night in a casino on the nearest reservation they doubled their budgets for this trip. Which is to say, they are more generous than usual. As if cued on five, six, seven, eight, and one, each places a hundred-dollar bill in the basket. They turn on their heels, basket behind their right thighs, and march off, swinging their arms. A pack of businessmen headed back to the convention center for their conference on banking or franchise ownership or executive leadership.

Rafa can still see their ties long after they've gone. The knots at their necks.

"Should we count it?" Rufina says.

He gathers the bills, flips through them. She watches him put half into his left front pocket, the other half into his right. He stuffs the rattle in his waistband and makes for the corner of the plaza, heads toward the canyon. Rufina is slow to follow, dragging her leg.

Two

As they roll the wagon home, Rufina wants to lie down in the middle of the road like she did when the mother returned without the Explorer. Her head pointing downhill. Rocks in her mouth.

It's difficult for her to walk. The pain in her hip is a splinter buried deep beyond reach. Her posture is suffering. She's folded forward into a shape meant for a letter of the alphabet, not for a woman's body. She relies, more than she ever has, on her cane.

In Rafa's ears, a hammer strikes. Or is it a gun firing, or flint striking? He keeps looking for where it originates, from which direction, but cannot locate it. There is the steady repetition of it.

As they pass through the woods, the walls of green

seem more narrow than they ever have. The river has a current. Cobwebs pull at the skin on their arms as they push back branches. A coyote flashes in front of them, darting through the clearing in the path. Another follows. Rufina stops. Counts them, four.

"You're going to make it," Rufina tells Rafa. He can't hear her over the noise in his ears. She does not say, "I won." She does not say, "I saved you."

As they approach the house, it prepares to gather them close. Somber as a house full of loss can be.

Three of the Grandmothers to All pass by on foot. They stop, let Rafa and Rufina cross. They have known them both since birth. There are soft hellos and watchful eyes. After Rafa and Rufina pass, the women turn to one another and sharply change direction. As they swiftly make for the compound, they've already made it through an initial draft of their plans.

Three

Officer Armijo had a dream the night before. It was not uncommon for Lucio to dream about dispatches before they were made. It was not uncommon for him to dream about a mountain lion cuffed in his backseat or losing his keys, a dream from which he'd wake and immediately be in a panic, ripping his pockets until he found them right where he'd left them before he'd gone to bed.

In the dream he'd had the night before, he'd been the first to respond to the call. Of course he knew the road. Of course he knew the canyon. Of course he knew the house. Could drive there without his lights on. When he arrived, the front door was open. He stepped through the house with his flashlight shining into each corner. He started with Rufina's room, and then scanned the kitchen, the living room, the dining room, the bathroom, and ended in Rosalinda's bedroom. There, from the vigas, hung both of them. He couldn't tell who'd gone first, or if they'd done it together. Their faces looked the exact same. It was clear whose children they were.

He left his wife in bed, stumbled to the kitchen sink, and poured himself a glass of water. He let the cold run up and down the insides of his forearms. He splashed his face. As he stood there dripping, he drank from the glass. Next, he looked in on his sons. All of them tucked onto their right sides, breathing their way through the murky depths of sleep.

On his way back through the kitchen, he saw the angel sitting on the counter, her impossible long legs. The smell of sour, oily feathers in need of fresh air.

"You may still have a chance," she said, putting a cherry Colt in the corner of her mouth. "For that rescue you've been fantasizing about." She leaned over to the stove, switching on the flame, and the tip lit immediately. "All these years you've been trying to atone for what was never up to you to prevent."

Lucio hung his head and turned away from her.

As the angel inhaled, the cigar crackled and hissed, as if it had its own opinion and finally wanted to share. She continued, "Listen carefully. At the base of the mulberry tree—"

At the mention of the tree, Lucio's shoulders began to quake, like earth does when it loosens as it yields to the shovel, sinking.

Four

The angel sits in the rocking chair on the roof, tapping her toes as she tilts forward and then back. She spies on Rafa, who is bent over the edge of the well. He lifts the lid, tugs at his pockets, dispenses each of the hundred-dollar bills into the dark, wet tunnel. Bends down, pries open the lid further.

The memory of his mother in the bath swarms his mind's eye. There, in the bathroom, the steam glistens on every surface. She has lit a bundle the Grandmothers to All gave her after they brought her back from the clinic. The abortion was a simple procedure and the only choice she could think to make. It was such a simple proce-dure, she can't imagine that it released what the Explorer planted inside her. The fumes from the bundle mix with the steam and fog the room. Rafa is on his knees on the tile beside the bath.

"Help me," she tells him. "You have to help me." She is furious in her scrubbing. Water splashes over the side of the tub, soaking his shirt and the thighs of his pants. The bar of soap, submerged between her legs, turns the water to milk. Suds ride the surface and slip over the edge.

He's nauseated from the bundle's scent.

"Give me your hands," she says, and when he does, she puts the soap in them. She is moving his hands between her legs. "Scrub harder," she says.

His hands are slipping. He doesn't know exactly where he's supposed to scrub. He tries to not feel with his hands.

"Harder," she cries.

He does as he's told. He leans into the tub. His T-shirt is soaked. His pants are soaked. His hair is dripping.

Suddenly, the mother stops. Water continues to slosh over the top. The floor is thoroughly puddled. She is trembling.

She sees what he hadn't noticed. He's hard. He doesn't want to be. He's sixteen. He prefers boys.

She is flailing as if a caught fish. The sounds she makes are not human. What he sees when she looks at him in that moment, he does not know, but from the look on her face, it is not human, either. He must not be human.

She didn't hear him saying he was sorry. She couldn't

have heard him with the commotion. He was punching his erection as she wailed.

Know this: It was Rafa who comforted her after she forced the Explorer to evacuate. She had chased him out of the house, down the lane, and out of the canyon with her hands clawing at the sky. Every rock within her reach was used to tell him no apology would suffice. And if she could've reached the sun, that immense flaming rock, she would've hurled that, too. There would be no forgiveness. He'd worshipped Rufina's body. He'd filled her with the essence of himself, too. How could he turn from Rosalinda, who he told was everything? Everything. Until she'd come to believe it. No other woman existed. There was no other body. No other port of entry to pleasure. And yet, she'd forgotten to see her growing daughter as another woman, with a body. And which like all bodies could be caressed, could be harmed, consumed.

The Explorer took nothing. All was left waiting in its place as he stumbled from the canyon, past city limits to the highway, and put out his thumb. There was no destination where he would be able to forget the house, the mother, the daughter, and what he'd left inside both. He hitched south, farther than he'd ever been before, and kept hitching south until he ran out of land.

For weeks following, Rosalinda mourned. On her bed, Rafa under the sheet with her like a cat. Petting his back with her feet. Tracing his hips with the tips of her toes. It was necessary for the mother to weep and wail. The records played, she puddled in her bed for days at a time. A candle dripped wax onto the wood floor, one after another. Cigarettes, one after another. All while down the hall, at the start of her second trimester, Rufina grew fat, like she had swallowed something without first chewing it and now there was only one way for it to come out. She prayed the Explorer would come back for her. Why couldn't she be treasured when her mother was? Was she not her mother's daughter? Nothing about hurt is rational. Which is to say, no matter Rosalinda's story, or Rufina's story, or the Explorer's story, which changed shape given the moment and the sensation, all loved and all lost. There was an act of violation and betrayal. And yet, who loved most? Who lost more?

Here is what you need to understand about a mother's love: It was Rosalinda that chose to have the life inside her cleaned out. The day after she found out about Rufina's pregnancy and chased the Explorer from the house, her legs were in stirrups at the clinic while the Grandmothers to All completed her paperwork at the front desk. Rosalinda had the abortion because she knew Rufina would need to heal and that the baby would give her that. After all, that was what Rafa had done, made living possible for her. She wanted to give this to her daughter.

Rafa watches the bills in the well soak through. He imagines a shoreline thirteen hundred miles away. Walking into the ocean, sand pulling at his feet.

He makes his way through the house, down the hall which to him feels like a thousand miles, a journey crossing continents. Once in the mother's room, he locks and bars the door. Pulls the curtains. He chooses the viga above. He places the chair beneath. Throws the rope. He steps up, makes his knot with as much reverence as a prayer. Then, the sound of her voice.

"*Mi conejito*," she says.

Finally, what he has sensed is clearly before him. The fins of her dress, the huipil wrapped at her shoulders, the headdress of mums. Her lips stained in fuchsia. The smell of her filling the room.

"I wouldn't go without you," she says.

"I can see you," he says. "I can hear you," he says, stepping off the chair and into her arms.

Five

The Explorer smelled of vinegar, curing meat, and fried apples. All that time in the kitchen preparing food for them. When he smiled, he appeared trustworthy. It was the way he raised his hairline, his forehead pitching upward, as if asking permission for his momentary happiness. He had trained Rufina to lean into his understanding of her, not develop her own. Only he knew the stories about who she was, where she came from. He gave Rufina to herself before the destruction of her people, and during the destruction, and after the destruction. History as if living in her. In this way, she could pretend she had been there right along with Rosalinda and had survived, too. It didn't matter that he'd researched it all in encyclopedias and in the Spanish newspapers. It didn't matter that it wasn't actually her people at all, but a combination of people he'd met stateside and interviewed. At a certain point, wasn't it all the same story? Couldn't Rosalinda have been any woman escaping from military dictatorship in Central America? What did Rufina know? What choice did she have but to see her mother as land from which she'd come? Study her as if she were a map she'd never understand? The sole carrier of their lineage, Rosalinda's womb, Rufina's homeland, and yet, see the separation. The perpetual loss of and longing for home.

He had been telling her a story as he'd done so many times before. She was wrapped in his arms as they both lay on her bed, which was not uncommon, a girl held by her father. This had been their routine for years. Only he was not her father. And at fourteen, she was the kind of girl who was plump to the pinch with full breasts and hips, already taller than her mother, as if she were the woman of the house. He had not been sleeping in Rosalinda's bed but had found himself back on the couch, outside. Their own intimacy happened in brief moments far from her bed, in the garden, in the parked car, next to the river. It was Rafa at sixteen who'd been waiting on his mother, lingering in her room until the late hours, crawling into her bed. Lighting her cigarettes, making her cups of hot ginger tea. Listening to her incomprehensible speech. The vigilant, devoted son.

It wasn't as if the Explorer had planned it. All he'd done was taken off his shoes and his socks. The story was about a jaguar priestess who could see in the dark. It wasn't that the story was funny, but she caught a spell of laughter and couldn't stop herself. It was the shaking her body made and the sounds of pleasure rubbing against him that made him kiss her. It was only the top of her head, and this was a familiar act, how many of these kisses before she threw her head forward to catch her breath and there was his mouth, found. His lips covering hers and he couldn't stop. There was no stopping. She kept her mouth open, which made him think something he never should have—that she was receptive to him. His pants were off. The sheets pulled back and her nightdress lifted to her neck. Why wasn't she wearing any under-wear? His hands between her legs did not have to fight. He never should have thought this was confirmation of desire, as she did not sleep with underwear, not since she stopped wetting the bed when she was four. The weight and fullness of him buried her. A man over six feet tall, over two hundred pounds. He pinned her and pulled at her like she was a woman who'd done this before, who'd expected it, not like she was the girl who he made break-fast for and whose temples he kissed.

Who had only wanted to please him.

Who had only wanted to be loved as much as the mother was loved.

Who couldn't see there at her window, Lucio, her sweet admirer, her want-to-be guardian as he cried. Covering his eyes because he could not summon the courage he needed to save her.

Who couldn't imagine all the women she was related to, who had come before her—tucked into their respective places in each of her cells—and had awoken and witnessed what was happening. Collectively, they shook their heads and collectively beat at their hearts. Wailing. Their voices were the music that spun Baby deep in Rufina, delivering her a talisman, which would keep her strong until the time came for her to deliver herself.

Six

✧

Lucio knocks at the door. He's unsure if anyone will answer. He's unsure if he's knocked loud enough. He is not in his uniform. It's his pickup truck, not the police car, in the drive. The monkey painted on the outside of the house has almost entirely faded. The tail is gone completely. The eyes are visible, two black points, a fan of leaves surround it, their tips sharp. The call did not come from the station. It came from the compound up the road, from the Grandmothers to All.

When Rufina appears, the hair at her temples and neck is damp with sweat, a braid slung over her shoulder. Her T-shirt and jeans, both white. She is barefoot. Her face, naked. She appears older than her age. She is forty-five, she is sixty, she is seventy-two. Her cane, her wooden companion, at her side. She has trouble looking Lucio in the eye. He notices how difficult it is for her to focus.

"He won't come out," she says to Lucio as if she were expecting him. "We made enough. I won." Her face is sunburned. The three days exposed on the plaza have made pink tracks down her nose and across her cheeks. "He won't come out," she says again.

Lucio does not know how to get her from the house into his car. The angel did not give him instructions. He is awkward, shifting like a high school boy from side to side. Then the father in him steps forward, takes both of her hands. Gently, he begins to lead her.

Rufina allows him. He sees defeat in her pupils. It's fixed there. She leaves the front door without her cane. One foot and then the other across the yard. When he has her in his truck, he returns to the house, grabs her purse just inside on the table, and her shoes. He follows the instruction he was given, lifts the rock at the base of the mulberry tree. There is the pack of smokes filled with bills, in addition to a damp stack still stinking like the well from which they came. Remember what is buried beneath this: the bones of Baby held in the sweet earth, always cherished. Holy in the way only the sweet earth can know and hold. Another seed to comfort.

Lucio makes a call up the road. Tells the Grand-mothers to All he's got her.

Sitting with her in the front seat, Lucio locks the doors, starts the engine. Rufina's breathing changes. Gathering air feels not unlike sipping it from a straw. Which is to say sometimes the hardest part about surviving is remembering to breathe.

The angel is still in the rocking chair on the roof. From this vantage point, she can see the truck with Rufina inside.

"I want you to listen to me very carefully," Lucio tells Rufina, putting the car in reverse. His voice is deliberate. "I am going to drive you to the airport. There will be a woman waiting. I am going to put you on a plane. She will get on with you."

Rufina's sips of air become more difficult. She can't get a full inhalation. She does not know who she is meant to be. Lucio keeps talking. Each of his words, a resting place. She tries to hold on.

The sun cuts through the windshield as Lucio drives west out of the canyon. While he squints into the sun, Rufina barely blinks. Arrangements have been made in quick succession. The Grandmothers to All have kin in cities all over the country. Women waiting to claim other women who are lost, refugees of one kind or another, the sole survivors of their families.

She is her mother. She is not her mother.

She will be ushered into the next decades of her life in a place where she has never been before. A place she knows nothing about. A place that will meet her and save her. As the right place can do. There will be the period of rehabilitation. Women who will feed her, instruct her on how to begin again, who will find her a home that knows how to hold her. There will be tinctures to stop the nightmares. There will be blankets to wrap her in.

In the rearview mirror, Lucio sees the Grandmothers to All coming down the road with sheets for wrapping the dead.

The steady sinking of the sun continues. The plaza is vacant. Set lights dimming. The shops closed. The hotels are momentarily hollow, waiting for the next arrivals. The Original Enduring Ones have packed up and gone. The portál where they've sat all weekend still radiates with the heat from their presence.

Once Lucio and Rufina pass through the last stoplight and veer onto the freeway, the road opens. The mountains are blue as the deep they were once submerged under. The land expands, infinite and holy, as the sky opens further, and the light.

The light, the light, the light.

Acknowledgments

No doubt with my best intentions, I will still miss those I wish I would have included here. Please accept my sincere apologies. A hundred thousand thank-you's to the following for all their generosity and support:

My agent, PJ Mark, whose presence, attention, and integrity are of the highest quality. I am forever grateful to you and all that you have done and continue to do. Thank you also to Ian Bonaparte (assistant extraordinaire). My editor, Jonathan Lee, thank you for exceeding all my expectations. What a joy to work with you. To everyone at Catapult—Alicia Kroell, Nicole Caputo, Wah-Ming Chang, Carla Bruce-Eddings, Katie Boland, Megan Fishmann, Rachel Fershleiser, Samm Saxby, Laura Gonzalez—and all other benevolent forces who had a hand in manifesting this dream, my deepest appreciation.

To those who provided the physical space of their homes for me to write the drafts of this book—Michelle Victoria, Katie Power, Rachel Balkcom and Ian Sanderson, Michael Waldron and Chantal Combes—many thanks. To those beloved beings whom I cherish and who also provided the sanctuary of space in addition to the never-ending resource of loving support—Toby Herzlich (Queen of the HEART and advocate of all things Mother Earth--om tare tuttare, ture so ha), Clara de la Torre (Bodhisattva and sister friend), Eileen Olivieri (fierce truth-teller and tender care-taker, you are a gift), Mark Hess (the brother I always wanted and never had, you are pure light), Colleen Kelly (my chosen auntie/mentor and example of life-long commitment to creative practice and honoring soul/spirit, I bow to you) and Katharine Menton (for all our life-times together and this one, too, such grace and the balm of belonging). A very special thank you to Ren Nelson who gifted a home/refuge for all those years for me to become the writer I am today. Your investment in me during that time is responsible for so much positive change in my life. And to anyone else who permitted me a table, a room, a safe space to continue drafting pages for however short the duration of time—my gratitude. To the Sierra Nevada College MFA Writer-in-Residency,

ACKNOWLEDGMENTS

Bread Loaf, VONA, the Jack Kent Cooke Graduate Arts Award, and the Rona Jaffe Foundation, thank you for choosing me.

For the early readers and all your brilliant insights—Kim Parko, Tomás Morín, William Shih, Elise Ota, Christopher Castellani, and Stephen Graham Jones. And to those who read late drafts and shared support at large, Tommy Orange and Tiphanie Yanique. Two incredible forces of magic who have changed my reality—for your mentorship, all your teaching/insights/example, for your inclusion of me, for your dear friendship, and for your imaginative force and books in the world, on my shelf, and close to my heart, Ramona Ausubel and Marie-Helene Bertino.

To all those who shared knowledge of the craft, assisted me with my writing and gave me the best experience of themselves, my teachers, a very humble thank you—with special recognition to Natalie Goldberg. To the entire community of the Institute of American Indian Arts, both the undergraduate and graduate faculty, visiting writers/professors, and students past and present—the biggest embrace. To the Lannan Foundation for all the readings, conversations, dinners, and time spent with extraordinary authors, thank you for your undeniable force for good in the world.

So many comadres, fellow visionaries, dearest friends/sisters to offer appreciation for (the short list)—Edie Tsong (+ Che!), Cristina González, Sydney Cooper (+ Lucio, inspiring namesake) (VIVA MEZCLA!), Chrissie Orr, and Molly Sturges, Adelma Hnasko, Annie Chamberlain, and Kelly Sue Enfield. To the entire WOC writing group, especially those who always showed up, no matter what—Beth Lee and Jennifer Love. Thank you all for your inspiration and unique ways in the world. For chosen family, spotlighting specifically, Ann Filemyr and Onde Chimes, my very young grannies.

To the incredible writing community of Santa Fe—too many to name here—whose work adds to the quality of daily living and pushing pen in this place of enchantment. To Littleglobe and the Santa Fe Art Institute who are committed to social justice and equitable, dignifying engagement, thank you for including me, for your work in the world, and in our community.

To my sister, Linda, thank you for being such a profound example of transformation. Healing can happen in one generation, and effect all generations to come, your love and your family are proof. To my mother who has tried her best, my stepfather Jim (Pa), and the rest of my motley crew of kin, thank you for doing your part.

To Mary Charles (legendary reader and learner) and Alecia Charles (your laugh is medicine), thank you for sharing your son and brother with me. Appreciate your support and sharing in this celebration.

And always, always, always, with my whole heart, with my whole being, thank you to my partner, Randle, and our son, Tsítso Kalaná.

© Zoë Zimmerman

JAMIE FIGUEROA received her MFA in creative writing from the Institute of American Indian Arts. Her writing has appeared in *Epoch, McSweeney's,* and *American Short Fiction*. She is the recipient of the Truman Capote Scholarship and is a Bread Loaf scholar. Boricua by way of Ohio, Figueroa lives in northern New Mexico.